She watched until Sawyer and his daughter had disappeared from her sight.

From her vantage point in the bedroom window, Amanda saw the backyard. There was an area of lush lawn, then the faint dark sparkle of swamp water surrounded by tangled vegetation and gnarled, twisted cypress trees.

A narrow, wooden dock with side rails extended out over the water, appearing to her as an invitation to an inhospitable wildness.

This was not a place of warmth and safety, but rather one of uncertainty with the potential for imminent danger. And if she listened to idle gossip, it was possible that the man was as dangerous as the place.

CARLA CASSIDY

HIS NEW NANNY

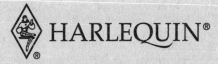
HARLEQUIN®

TORONTO • NEW YORK • LONDON
AMSTERDAM • PARIS • SYDNEY • HAMBURG
STOCKHOLM • ATHENS • TOKYO • MILAN • MADRID
PRAGUE • WARSAW • BUDAPEST • AUCKLAND

ISBN-13: 978-0-373-69285-9
ISBN-10:   0-373-69285-4

HIS NEW NANNY

This edition published by arrangement with Harlequin Books S.A.

ABOUT THE AUTHOR

Carla Cassidy is an award-winning author who has written over fifty novels for Silhouette Books. In 1995 she won Best Silhouette Romance from *Romantic Times BOOKreviews* for *Anything for Danny*. In 1998 she also won a Career Achievement Award for Best Innovative Series from *Romantic Times BOOKreviews*.

Carla believes the only thing better than curling up with a good book to read is sitting down at the computer with a good story to write. She's looking forward to writing many more books and bringing hours of pleasure to readers.

Books by Carla Cassidy

HARLEQUIN INTRIGUE
379—PASSION IN THE FIRST DEGREE
411—SUNSET PROMISES*
415—MIDNIGHT WISHES*
419—SUNRISE VOWS*
447—THEIR ONLY CHILD
498—A FATHER'S LOVE
1018—HIS NEW NANNY

*Cheyenne Nights

CAST OF CHARACTERS

Sawyer Bennett—Was he an innocent man or guilty of a heinous crime?

Amanda Rockport—She'd come to Conja Creek to escape her past, only to find herself a pawn in somebody's deadly game.

Molly Bennett—The little girl quit talking on the night she saw her mother murdered. When she finally speaks, will she name the murderer?

George Carlyle—A handyman with secrets.

Helen—The Bennett housekeeper. Was the Bennett family her deadly obsession?

Adam Kincaid—Sawyer's business partner. Did his ambition lead him to murder?

James and Lillian Cordell—Sawyer's neighbors. Did their friendliness hide ulterior motives?

Chapter One

"They say he killed his wife." The old man's grizzled eyebrows drew together in a frown. "Killed her then tried to feed her to the gators."

Amanda Rockport stared at him, unsure if he was pulling her leg. "Then why isn't he in jail?" she asked.

"Circumstantial evidence, but not enough proof to put the man behind bars. Besides, he's rich. Money talks and the guilty walks. You best go back to where you came from and leave Sawyer Bennett to the devil where he belongs."

Amanda fought the impulse to reach up and rub the center of her forehead where a tension headache had lived for the past month.

"I've never been one to put much stock in idle gossip," she replied. She wished she hadn't stopped in the small café before reaching her final destination—Sawyer Bennett's home.

She cupped her hands around the hot cup of coffee and considered doing exactly what the old man had suggested, going back to where she'd come from.

Unfortunately that really wasn't an option. She'd used the last of her money to travel from Kansas City to Conja Creek, Louisiana. Besides, there was nothing left for her in Kansas City.

She finished her coffee and stood. "I appreciate the advice," she said to the old man who had sat on the stool next to her at the café counter.

His blue eyes gazed at her sharply. "You're making a mistake."

"I guess it's my mistake to make." She threw a couple of dollars on the counter to pay for the coffee. As she stepped out of the café, the hot, humid air hit her like a slap in the face and half stole her breath.

She moved quickly to her car, where she started the engine and waited for cool air to blow from the vents. "They say he killed his wife." The old man's words echoed in her head.

Surely Johnny wouldn't have arranged this job for her if he'd thought Sawyer Bennett was a danger. Granted her brother didn't always exhibit the best judgment, but there was no way he'd send her to work for a murderer.

All Johnny had told her when he'd approached her about the job was that Sawyer Bennett had been a college roommate and the two men had stayed in touch over the years and that Sawyer had lost his wife recently and needed a nanny.

Think of the child, she told herself. Think of Melanie. She opened the file folder on the seat next to her and withdrew the photo of the little girl. She looked small for her age, and her eyes radiated a sadness too profound for an eight-year-old.

She knew from her brief correspondence with Sawyer Bennett that two months ago Melanie Bennett had gone mute.

With Amanda's psychology degree and teaching background, she'd felt confident that she'd be able to help Melanie. And any job that got her away from the mess of her life in Kansas City had been appealing. Until she'd stopped for coffee and made the mistake of passing time with an old-timer seated next to her.

Now a rumble of apprehension thundered through her head, intensifying her headache. At the moment she really had no choice. She couldn't go back. She could only go forward and hope that she wasn't making a monumental mistake.

With a deep breath, she backed out of the parking space. Sawyer's directions had indicated that she'd pass through the town of Conja Creek. She *should* have passed through. She should have never stopped for that coffee.

She left the town behind and turned down a narrow road flanked by trees dripping moss. The sunlight seemed to disappear as if unable to penetrate the depths of the surrounding forest.

Clutching the steering wheel more tightly, she

found the alien landscape both forbidding and fascinating. A twist here, a turn there and she came to a clearing. The large plantation-style house filled the space, flanked by tall trees and backed by the swamp.

It was an impressive structure, with thick white columns and a sweeping veranda that seemed to go on forever. It didn't whisper of old money, it screamed it.

She parked next to a black pickup and cut the engine, but was reluctant to leave the familiar confines of her car. They say he killed his wife and fed her to the gators. Nothing but rumor, she told herself. And she knew all about rumors and innuendoes.

She knew all about circumstantial evidence and that sometimes it had nothing to do with truth. It had been circumstantial evidence and rumors that had destroyed her life.

It didn't take long for the car to get too hot, so she grabbed her purse and the file folder and got out. The air hung heavy, the humidity nearly visible as she headed toward the stairs that led to the porch. The silence was as oppressive as the air.

Please don't let this be a mistake, she mentally begged. She needed this job. She needed this child in order for her to redeem herself. Drawing on the inner strength that had left her for the past couple of months, she knocked on the door.

The door creaked open, and Amanda found herself face-to-face with Melanie. The little girl's brown eyes widened. She turned on her heels and raced away.

"Wait! Melanie," Amanda said, taking a step into the entry, but the child raced around a corner and disappeared.

"You must forgive my daughter. She was expecting somebody else and doesn't do well with strangers." The deep voice came from the doorway opposite the direction in which Melanie had run.

Amanda recognized the voice from the single phone conversation she'd had with him. She turned to face Sawyer Bennett.

She wasn't sure what she'd expected, but he wasn't it. She hadn't anticipated the broad shoulders that stretched the black T-shirt he wore. She hadn't expected him to be so tall. But more than anything she hadn't anticipated the handsome, haunted features; the black hair or the dark green eyes that reminded her of a mysterious forest.

"I wasn't sure you'd come and so I didn't prepare Melanie for your arrival," he said. "I'm Sawyer Bennett." He stepped closer to her and held out a hand. "And I assume you're Amanda."

She nodded, shook his hand and tried not to notice the scent that drifted off him, the scent of something wild and slightly intoxicating. "It's nice to meet you," she said as he dropped her hand and stepped back.

"I trust you had no problems finding the place?"

She thought about telling him she'd stopped into the café in Conja Creek but then changed her mind. "Your directions were excellent," she replied. "I had no trouble."

"Good. Then we'll just get you settled in. If you'll follow me I'll show you to the room where you'll be staying."

Amanda had always considered herself pretty good at reading people, but she found it impossible to read her new employer. She followed him up the stairs, trying to absorb the first impressions that filled her head.

The house was silent except for their footsteps whispering against the plush beige carpeting, but there was a simmering energy that pulsed in the air, and she wasn't sure if it radiated from the house itself or the man in front of her.

Please don't let this be a mistake. The mantra repeated itself in her head as she stared at his stiff, unyielding back. They reached the top of the stairs and passed a closed door. He stepped into the next room and gestured her inside.

It was a pleasant bedroom decorated in various shades of yellow. "You can stay in here or you're welcome to one of the other guest bedrooms. Melanie's room is right next door to this one and the only drawback is that you'll share a bathroom with her."

As Amanda looked through the bathroom she saw Melanie peeking around the corner. Her little gamin face was there only a moment, then gone. "I certainly don't mind if Melanie doesn't. This will be just fine."

He nodded. "I assume you have suitcases in your

car? If you'll give me the key I'll see that they're brought up to you."

"I'd like to go over the particulars," she began as she handed him her keys, but he held up a hand to stop her.

"We'll talk later. I know you've had a long trip. Dinner is at six. We'll talk after that." He didn't wait for her response, but instead turned on his heels and left her alone in the room.

She heard the murmur of his deep voice and when she looked into the hallway she saw Sawyer and his daughter, her little hand in his, going back down the stairs. She watched until they disappeared from sight, then she walked to the mirror above the dresser to see if the apprehension that fluttered in her chest showed on her face.

Her blue eyes reflected none of the turmoil, and her dark brown hair remained pulled back away from her features in a low ponytail that went to the middle of her shoulders. She'd worn no makeup, hoping that without it she would look older than her twenty-seven years.

She knew that Sawyer was thirty-three, the same age as her brother, and she hadn't wanted him to think of her as Johnny's baby sister.

She turned away from the mirror with a small sigh and instead walked over to the bedroom window and peered outside.

From this vantage point she saw the backyard. There was an area of lush lawn, then the faint dark sparkle of swamp water surrounded by tangled vegetation and gnarled, twisted cypress trees.

A narrow wooden dock with side rails extended out over the water, appearing to her as an invitation to an inhospitable wildness.

This was not a place of warmth and safety, but rather one of uncertainty with the potential for imminent danger. With an eight-year-old living here, there should be laughter and chatter. The house should teem with noise, but instead the utter silence pressed in around her. And if she listened to idle gossip it was possible that the man was as dangerous as the place.

She couldn't think that way. She refused to let the words of a stranger in a café override her brother's characterization of Sawyer Bennett. Still, she wished she'd done a little research before jumping at the job opportunity.

She knew Sawyer Bennett was an architect, but surely he had people who worked for him here in the house. A cook, a housekeeper, some people to work the grounds. She couldn't imagine living in a place this size without having a staff of some sort. So, where was everyone?

She didn't know how long she'd been standing at the window, staring out and wondering what she'd gotten herself into, when a loud thump resounded from behind her.

She whirled around to see a burly blond man just inside her room. He'd dropped her large suitcase on the floor and still held her smaller overnight bag. "Name is George. I work for Mr. Bennett." He placed the overnight bag on the floor and when he straightened, his gaze swept her from head to toe. "Be nice to have something pretty to look at again."

Something about his gaze made her feel like she needed a shower, but before she could say anything he turned and left. She rubbed the center of her forehead where the tension headache had renewed its acquaintance with her.

What in the heck had she gotten herself into?

At quarter to six Amanda left her bedroom and headed down the stairs in search of the dining room or kitchen. In the two hours she'd been in her room she'd unpacked her things, taken a shower and changed her clothes. In that time she'd heard nothing, seen nobody.

As she descended, the scent of something savory cooking made her stomach rumble in response, reminding her she hadn't eaten since that morning.

But more than appease her hunger, she was eager to spend some time with Melanie, anxious to learn more about what, exactly, her nanny job entailed.

She ran her hands down the sides of her navy dress, hoping she was dressed appropriately. When he'd indicated that dinner was at six, she'd had the feeling that jeans and a T-shirt were not appropriate attire.

She found Melanie seated next to her father on the

sofa in the living room. Sawyer rose to his feet as she entered. "Good evening, Ms. Rockport." She was grateful she'd decided to wear the dress, as he was clad in a pair of dress slacks and a crisp white shirt.

"Please, make it Amanda," she replied and smiled at Melanie.

"This is my daughter," Sawyer said. "Melanie, this is the woman I told you about. She's going to take care of you."

"I hope we'll be friends," Amanda said.

Melanie stared at her warily, then gave a curt nod of her head. This was a child who would not trust easily, Amanda thought. It was going to take time and patience to earn her trust.

"I've invited some friends to join us for dinner," Sawyer said. "James and Lillian Cordell. Lillian went to high school with my wife and they're Melanie's godparents and good friends. They should be arriving anytime. They live in the house closest to us." He gestured her toward a chair across from the sofa.

Again she noticed the seething, just-below-the-surface energy that emanated from him, which slightly repelled and attracted her. She had so many questions for him about her position here, but it seemed as if none of them would be answered until after dinner.

Before any conversation could continue, the doorbell rang and Sawyer got up to answer, leaving Melanie and Amanda alone. Melanie stared at her folded hands in her lap. A sadness about her made

Amanda want to join Melanie on the sofa and wrap her in a tight, loving embrace.

Instead she softly spoke her name, and Melanie looked up at her. "I know it's kind of scary to meet new people," Amanda said. "But I think we're going to get along just fine. I don't know about you, but I like to do all kinds of things." Melanie tilted her head quizzically and Amanda continued. "I like to draw and I love to color. I like to tell stories and play dress up. I like to have tea parties and sometimes I even like to collect bugs."

One corner of Melanie's lips twitched upward in a faint smile. *It's a start,* Amanda told herself. Now if she could just get even a half smile out of Sawyer Bennett she might feel a little bit at ease.

He returned to the living room with an attractive couple. "James, Lillian, I'd like to introduce you to my new nanny, Amanda Rockport."

Amanda stood and smiled. "Nice to meet you both," she said.

"It's wonderful to meet you," Lillian exclaimed and took Amanda's hand in hers. "It will be so nice to have woman conversation again." She released Amanda's hand and went directly to Melanie. "And there's my girl," she said, and pulled Melanie into a tight embrace. Melanie returned the embrace, then stepped back.

"Dinner is ready, so we can go on into the dining room," Sawyer said.

Sawyer sat at the head of the table with Melanie on

his right and Amanda on his left. Lillian sat next to Amanda and James sat at the opposite end of the table.

An elderly woman Sawyer introduced to Amanda as Helen served them. Her sharp gaze perused Amanda as if taking stock of her character. Once the meal was served she silently disappeared back into the kitchen.

It would have been easy for Amanda to feel out of place. Melanie remained silent as did Sawyer, but the blond, vivacious Lillian engaged Amanda in conversation immediately.

"So, where are you from?" Lillian asked Amanda as Lillian buttered a biscuit the size of her fist.

"Kansas City," Amanda replied.

Lillian looked at Sawyer in surprise. "How on earth did you find her?"

"Amanda's brother and I went to college together," Sawyer said. "I mentioned to him that I was in the market for a nanny, and it just so happened that Amanda was in the market for a job."

"You know I was perfectly happy taking care of Melanie," Lillian exclaimed. "We had lots of fun, didn't we, sweetheart?" She smiled at Melanie, who replied with a quick nod of her head.

"I couldn't allow you to continue to ignore your own work," Sawyer said smoothly. He looked at Amanda, those dark green eyes of his enigmatic. "Lillian is an artist who has neglected her work for the past couple of months to help me out with Melanie."

"An artist? What kind of art?" Amanda asked.

"I dabble in a little bit of everything," she replied.

"She's being modest." James looked at his wife affectionately. "One of the things she 'dabbles' in is making Mardi Gras masks that are unbelievable. People come from all over the country to buy a Lillian mask for the celebration."

It didn't take long for Melanie to finish eating and look at her father with pleading eyes. He told her she was dismissed from the table, and it seemed she couldn't escape the room of grown-ups fast enough.

"Poor little thing," Lillian said when she was gone. "My heart just aches for her."

"She'll be fine," Sawyer replied. "With Amanda here we can establish a routine and before long she'll be back to her old self." He said it forcefully, as if by sheer willpower alone he could make it so.

Once again Amanda wondered under what circumstances Melanie had stopped speaking. Was it grief over her mother's death that had stolen her desire to talk? She couldn't wait until dinner was over and the Cordells had gone home so she and Sawyer could have a conversation about the daily work schedule and Melanie.

"You must let me show you around Conja Creek," Lillian said to Amanda. "I can show you the best place to have your hair done, what shop carries the best clothes in town and where all the ladies have lunch."

"I don't know how much time I'll have to shop or do lunch," Amanda replied. "My number-one priority is, of course, Melanie."

"As it should be," Lillian replied. "But surely you'll have some time off." She turned her attention to Sawyer. "You mustn't be a slave driver, Sawyer."

"I have no intention of that," he replied. "Amanda and I will work out an agreeable schedule that I'm sure will allow her to do whatever it is you ladies like to do in your spare time."

"Shop," James said, once again casting an affectionate gaze at his wife. "That's what my Lilly likes to do."

"And you wouldn't have it any other way," she replied with a laugh.

As Amanda watched the loving interplay between James and Lillian, she felt a pang of wistfulness. She'd thought she'd had that kind of relationship with Scott, but when her life had fallen apart he'd run as fast as he could from her.

"Conja Creek. It's an interesting name," Amanda said.

"Conja is Cajun and it means to put a spell on," Sawyer replied.

"Legend has it that the creek bewitches people, puts a spell on them and they never want to leave," Lillian said. "Personally, the creek hasn't gotten to me. I could move out of here tomorrow if my dear husband would. I'd love the hustle and bustle of Shreveport."

"Ah, but remember, here you're a big fish in a little pond and in Shreveport you'd be a little fish in a big pond," James teased.

Dinner might have been pleasant if Amanda hadn't been so aware of the simmering tension that seemed to be in the air around Sawyer. More than once throughout the meal she felt his gaze lingering on her, making her incredibly self-conscious and ill at ease.

It was after eight when the Cordells finally left and Sawyer led Amanda into his study. "I'll be right back. I need to check on Melanie," he said, and left her alone in the room.

A large desk dominated the space with what appeared to be a state-of-the-art computer on top. Several overstuffed chairs sat in front of the desk. Amanda sank into one of them, fighting the exhaustion that threatened to overwhelm her.

As she waited for Sawyer she looked around the room. One of the walls was decorated with framed photographs of buildings and homes. She assumed he'd been the architect on the projects.

Another wall held personal pictures, and she stood and moved closer to get a better view of these. There were several of Melanie. They looked to be school portraits, each one showing her a little older.

Then there were a couple of photographs of Sawyer, the woman who must have been his wife and Melanie. The woman was beautiful, a brunette with exotic dark eyes and lush lips. On the surface the photos depicted a happy family, but as Amanda studied the subtle body language, she saw a distance between husband and wife.

A distance that had resulted in murder?

There was one other picture that Amanda instantly recognized. Her brother had one just like it hanging on the wall in his office. The photo was of six young men, their arms slung around each other in easy friendship.

Amanda knew it had been taken in college. "The Brotherhood," Johnny had told her when she'd asked about it. He'd explained that the Brotherhood had been a group of young, wealthy men all from Conja Creek.

Johnny, who hadn't been from Conja Creek and had been at the college on a scholarship had been welcomed into the fold when he'd been assigned a room with Jackson Burdeaux, one of the men in the photo.

She sat in the chair again once more wondering if she had done the right thing in coming here. Certainly Lillian and James Cordell had seemed like respectable, decent people. Surely if they thought Sawyer Bennett had killed his wife they wouldn't be coming over for dinner.

She straightened in the chair, tension coiling in her stomach as Sawyer returned to the room. Each time she saw him she was struck again by the attractiveness of his bold features, his chiseled jaw and thick black hair.

"I think it would be easiest if I tell you my expectations. Then if you have a problem we can discuss it." His firm tone made her suspect he was not a man who was accustomed to having his authority questioned.

She nodded and waited for him to continue. He moved behind the desk and sat, his gaze direct and focused on her. "I need you to be here Monday through Friday from the time Melanie wakes up until she goes to bed. I have an office in Baton Rouge and will be driving back and forth on those days. You can have the weekends off." A smile curved the corners of his lips. "You'll be free to run the streets of Conja Creek with Lillian."

The magnetism of his smile caused a small ball of heat to ignite in the pit of her stomach. The smile was there only a moment, then gone. "What Melanie needs right now more than anything is routine and consistency. She needs somebody she can count on, somebody she can trust, and I'm hoping you can be that person for her."

She nodded. They had already discussed salary in their e-mail conversations, so nothing he'd said so far was a surprise. "I'm hoping Melanie and I will become the best of friends."

He stood as if to dismiss her. "We'll take things on a day-to-day basis. I won't keep you this evening. I know it's been a long day for you, and Melanie is an early riser. One last thing. My daughter is afraid of the dark. There's a night-light in her room. Make sure it's turned on each night when she goes to bed."

She got up from her chair, aware that she was being dismissed. "Before I leave, there's something

I'd like to ask you. I understand that Melanie quit speaking two months ago. Can you tell me under what circumstances this happened?"

He walked around the desk and moved to stand before her…too close…invading her space. His green eyes gleamed with a hard light as his lips once again curved into a smile, this one not so pleasant.

"Haven't you heard?" he asked, and one of his dark brows quirked upward. "Melanie stopped speaking on the night that I murdered her mother."

Chapter Two

Sawyer saw the lift of her chin that displayed a touch of bravado, which was incongruent with the loss of color from her face. She was a pretty woman, with her soft brown hair and guileless blue eyes. She smelled like jasmine, and he felt a stirring deep inside him as he breathed in her fragrance.

"If you're trying to shock me, then you've failed," she said. "I stopped at a café on my way here and heard all the rumors about your being responsible for your wife's murder."

"Then why did you come? Why didn't you high-tail it out of here when you heard the rumors?"

Some of the color was slowly returning to her cheeks. "Because Melanie needs somebody. Because my brother told me you're a good man."

The knot of tension that had been in his chest for weeks eased somewhat at her words. He'd always believed he was a good man, but Erica's murder had turned him into somebody he scarcely recognized.

"I didn't kill her." The words came from him without passion. "But I need to know how strong you are, if you can withstand the rumors, the absolute ugliness this has brought into this house, into my life. I don't want Melanie to get attached, then you wind up running because you can't take the heat."

Her chin tilted upward once again. "I have no intention of going anywhere until you tell me to go."

He nodded, satisfied with her answer, at least for the moment. "The investigation into Erica's death is ongoing. I will tell you that I'm the primary suspect right now."

"You said that Melanie stopped speaking that night. Could you tell me what happened? It would help me to understand her a little better."

Frantic worry stabbed through him as he thought of his daughter. What had she seen that night from her bedroom window? If she finally started speaking again, what would she be able to tell the authorities?

"I can't tell you exactly what happened. All I know is the night of Erica's murder I had fallen asleep right here in my office chair and a scream woke me. I knew instantly that it was Melanie. I raced upstairs and into her bedroom and found her standing in front of the window. She was sobbing and shaking so hard she could barely speak. She pointed out the window and said, 'Mommy's gone.'"

Amanda's face reflected the horror he'd felt that night as he continued. "I looked out the window to where she was pointing. There was a full moon that night, and on the dock I could see one of Erica's shoes and the lightweight wrap she often pulled on when she was going outside. I thought she'd fallen off the dock and into the swamp water. It wasn't until I ran down there to see if I could find her that I saw the blood and knew it hadn't been a simple fall."

He drew a deep breath, feeling the need for a drink, wanting to numb himself against the memories, both of Erica's life and her death.

"So, you don't know what Melanie saw?"

He shook his head. "I don't know exactly what she saw, but it frightened her so badly it stole her ability to talk. She hasn't said a single word since that night."

Suddenly exhausted, he moved toward the door. All he wanted at the moment was a drink, then to sleep without dreams. And he needed to get away from Ms. Amanda Rockport with her pleasing scent and cupid lips that reminded him it had been a long time since he'd enjoyed the pleasure of a woman. He'd stopped sleeping with Erica long before her death two months ago.

"As you can see, there's a computer in here. Feel free to use it during the hours I'm gone if you want to keep up with e-mail or whatever. If you need something for Melanie, just let me know and we'll get it. There's a phone in your room with a separate number from the house phone for your convenience." He rattled off the number, then gestured her out of the office. "And now, unless you have other questions, it's been a long day."

She walked in front of him, her slender hips swaying slightly beneath the navy dress she wore. "Will I see you in the morning?" she asked as she paused at the foot of the stairs leading up to the bedrooms.

"Probably not. I'll leave early to drive into Baton Rouge for a day at the office. I'll be home for dinner. If you need anything or have questions, Helen, our cook, will be able to help you."

"Then I guess I'll just say good-night," she replied.

He stood at the bottom of the stairs and watched her ascend. Something about her looked fragile, a shadow in her eyes, a touch of sadness to her features.

He hoped she was stronger than she looked, because he needed somebody strong and determined to stand by Melanie. He needed somebody who wouldn't be chased away by rumors and a murder case that seemed to point a finger at nobody but him.

When she'd disappeared from his sight, he returned to his office and pulled a bottle of Scotch and a glass from his bottom drawer. He poured a liberal amount, then sat back in his chair and took a sip, enjoying the smooth warmth that slid down his throat.

This was what he'd done on the night of Erica's murder. He'd sat in here and had drunk Scotch and seethed and stewed. He'd imagined his life without her, and the vision had been pleasing.

He'd been sick of her lies, the cheating and the knowledge that, not only was she tired of playing wife, she'd been tired of playing mommy. It had been that night that he'd made the decision to get her out of his life.

He now downed the Scotch and got up from the chair. He shut off the light in the office, then walked to the living room and stepped out of the French doors that led to the stone patio.

The moon had been full that night, and it was full again tonight. From this vantage point he could see the dock extending out over the glittering swamp. The hanging moss from the cypress trees appeared like gigantic silvery webs spun by gargantuan spiders.

The swamp was never silent. Insects buzzed and clicked a nighttime melody that had become as familiar to him as his own heartbeat.

His thoughts went back to the woman he'd invited into his home, into his daughter's life. Amanda Rockport wasn't what he'd been expecting. She was prettier than he'd imagined, not that he had any interest in pursuing anything romantic with her. She was his daughter's nanny and nothing else.

He smiled with a touch of bitterness. Now wouldn't that just set the local tongues wagging. He could just hear them speculating that he'd gotten rid of one woman to make room for another.

His smile faded. The way things were looking, he wouldn't have time to stir up more rumors or start a relationship. The way things were looking, it was very possible he was going to spend the rest of his life in prison for Erica's murder.

DESPITE THE LONG DRIVE the day before and the equally long evening, Amanda awakened early the next morning. The stress of a new place and a new bed to get used to hadn't stopped her from sleeping well. She got out of bed and padded over to the window where the sun had yet to climb completely above the tops of the trees.

Vapor rose from the water, shrouding the swamp in a haunting mist. Kansas City, Missouri, didn't have these kinds of views. It was a sober reminder to her that she was far away from home and dependent on a man who may or may not have murdered his wife.

She shook her head as if to dislodge this thought and instead left the window and crept through the bathroom and paused at Melanie's bedroom doorway.

The little girl was asleep, burrowed beneath the pink ruffled bedspread with only the top of her head showing. Amanda softly closed the door of the bathroom, then took a quick shower.

When she was finished and dressed in a pair of jeans and a light blue T-shirt, it was just after seven. She checked in on Melanie once again. Seeing that she was still asleep, Amanda crept down the stairs.

There were two things she wanted…coffee and information and not necessarily in that order. Assuming that Sawyer had already left, she went into his office. Even though he'd given her permission to use the computer, she felt like an intruder as she sat in his chair and punched the power button.

As she waited for the computer to boot up she was aware of the scent of him lingering in the room. A combination of earthy cologne, of shaving cream and the underlying wisp of some kind of alcohol.

Last night she'd wanted to ask him more questions about the murder, but there had been something slightly forbidding in his eyes.

When the computer was up and running she went to a search engine and punched in the words *Erica Bennett* and *murder.* The search yielded half a dozen results, all from the *Conja Creek Gazette.*

The first article she pulled up was the initial report of the murder. It was brief, telling only that the body of Erica Bennett had been pulled out of the swamp and foul play was suspected.

The second article detailed the crime more completely. Erica Bennett had been stabbed six times before being shoved or falling into the swamp. She had been pregnant at the time of her murder. Sawyer Bennett was being questioned about the death of his wife. The rest of the articles indicated the investigation was ongoing and no arrests had been made.

Amanda leaned back in the chair, stunned by the knowledge that Erica had been stabbed, and equally surprised that she'd been pregnant. So Sawyer hadn't only lost his wife, but he'd lost an unborn child, as well.

She shut down the computer, her mind whirling

as she headed for the kitchen to find a cup of coffee. Helen stood at the stove. Her eyes narrowed slightly as Amanda entered the room.

"If you'll take a seat in the dining room, I'll serve you breakfast," she said, no trace of friendliness in her voice.

"I'm not much of a breakfast eater and I'm not a guest. I work here, so I'll just have my coffee in here." She pointed to the round oak kitchen table.

"Suit yourself," Helen replied, pulling a cup from the cabinet. She filled it with coffee, then set it in front of Amanda at the table.

Amanda slid into one of the chairs and watched the old woman as she began to peel carrots at the sink. "Have you worked here a long time, Helen?" she asked.

"Long enough," Helen replied, offering no more information. Amanda took a sip of the coffee and stared out the window, where again she could see the place where Erica Bennett had lost her life.

"So, you knew Erica?" she finally asked.

"If you want gossip you've come to the wrong place." Helen turned to look at her. "I don't carry tales, and even if I did, I don't know you well enough to talk about personal things. For all I know you'll be gone tomorrow."

"I have no intention of going anywhere," Amanda countered.

Helen's gray eyes studied her coldly. "Time will tell. Death came calling at this house and I got a feeling in my bones that bad things are still to come. I figure you'll be out of here within a week." She turned back to the sink.

Amanda took another drink of her coffee. She'd hoped to make an ally of Helen, but it appeared that wasn't going to happen. She was truly on her own.

At that moment Melanie came into the kitchen. Still clad in her pajamas, her dark hair sleep tousled, she offered Amanda a shy smile, then slid into the chair opposite her at the table.

"There's my darlin'," Helen said, her gaze warm as it lingered on Melanie. "How about some French toast this morning?"

So the old woman had a soft spot, and that spot seemed to be Melanie, Amanda mused. Perhaps her unfriendliness toward Amanda was because she was afraid Amanda would get close to Melanie, then leave.

"Did you sleep well?" Amanda asked Melanie. Melanie nodded. "After you eat breakfast and get dressed, we'll talk about what we're going to do today."

The day passed surprisingly quickly. After breakfast and getting Melanie washed and dressed for the day, the two of them played an educational game that Amanda had brought with her.

Even though Melanie didn't say a word, Amanda recognized that the child was bright and had a good sense of humor. She also noticed that Melanie was eager to please, and when she did something wrong she flinched, as if anticipating a blow.

It concerned Amanda and she made a note to discuss it with Sawyer. Lunch was a picnic on the back patio. After they ate, they went for a walk, where Amanda kept up a running commentary about the bugs they encountered.

They were returning to the house when they met George, who carried a green-stained machete and whose gaze swept over Amanda. Melanie immediately drew closer to Amanda, her little body tense.

"Well, well, if it isn't Little Bit and the new nanny." He swung the machete up over his shoulder. "Getting settled in all right?"

"Fine, thank you," Amanda replied, and placed a hand on Melanie's shoulder.

He wiped a hand across his broad brow, where sweat trickled down. "You need somebody to show you around town, Ms. Nanny, you just call on me. Erica, she liked the places I took her."

A deep chill swept through Amanda. "Thank you, George, but I doubt I'll have time to do much sightseeing. Come on, Melanie, we'd better get inside and get cleaned up for dinner."

As they walked away, Amanda could still feel George's gaze burning into her back as his words whirled around in her head. Did George have something to do with Erica's murder? How dangerous was the handyman?

Sawyer didn't make it home in time for supper. She and Melanie ate in the kitchen and after dinner played another board game.

It was almost eight when Sawyer walked into Melanie's bedroom where the two were stretched out on the floor. Amanda quickly got to her feet as Melanie ran to her father and threw her arms around his waist.

If Amanda had any concerns about Sawyer being abusive with his daughter, they were dispelled as she saw the fierce love that lit Melanie's eyes as she hugged her daddy.

Amanda tried to ignore the faint tension that curled in the pit of her stomach at the sight of him. He looked unbelievably handsome in black slacks and a white shirt. His sleeves were rolled up to expose muscled forearms dusted with dark hair.

The last thing she needed was to develop a crush on her employer, especially a man who had a dark cloud of suspicion hanging over his head. Besides, even if he was innocent, he was a wealthy man who certainly wouldn't look for a wife among the hired help.

But she couldn't ignore the way her heartbeat accelerated and a slight breathlessness swept over her whenever he looked at her.

"And now it's bath time for you, my little one. While you take your bath and get ready for bed I'm going to see if Helen left me something to eat, then I'll be back up to tuck you in." He straightened and looked at Amanda. "And after I tuck in Melanie, I'd like to see you in my office."

It was almost nine when Sawyer ushered Amanda into his office and gestured her toward the chair in front of the desk. He'd changed from his slacks and dress shirt into a pair of jeans and a T-shirt that hugged his muscled chest.

"You don't look any the worse for wear after today," he observed as he sat behind the desk.

"We got along just fine," she assured him. "She's very bright."

His eyes gleamed with pride. "She is, but equally important is the fact that she has a loving heart." The light in his eyes was doused as quickly as it had shone. "I'm assuming you didn't get her to talk."

"I didn't try to get her to talk," Amanda replied. "Melanie has no reason to trust me right now, and the last thing I want to do is push her to do something she obviously doesn't want to do."

He leaned forward and for a moment his eyes shimmered with such torment she felt it deep inside of her. "Then why doesn't she trust me? She must know I'd never hurt her, that I love her more than anyone else on the face of the earth."

The momentary vulnerability on his features ripped through her, and she wanted to grab his hand, stroke his brow, give him a comforting touch. But she didn't. Instead she leaned back in the chair to distance herself from the impulse.

"I can't answer that, Sawyer. Elective muteness is difficult to understand and we can't know what's going on inside Melanie's head." She frowned, realizing she sounded clinical and detached. "She'll talk, Sawyer. When she's ready she'll talk, but Melanie is the one in control of that, and we just have to be patient."

The moment of vulnerability disappeared as his eyes glittered once again. "Patience has never been one of my strengths. I want what I want when I want it." The strength of the statement coupled with his gaze, which seemed to linger on her lips, caused her breath to catch in her chest.

"Unfortunately, you aren't in control of this situation," she replied, hoping she didn't reveal how she felt. She straightened in the chair. "I read the news reports about your wife's murder."

She wasn't sure why, but she felt the need to interject his wife into the conversation, needed to remind herself that he was a grieving man rather than an attractive, single hunk ready for a relationship.

Before he could reply, a scream pierced the air.

Chapter Three

Sawyer shot out of the chair and raced from the room. He knew that scream. Oh, God, but he knew that scream. *Melanie!* He took the stairs two at a time, vaguely aware of Amanda hurrying behind him.

His heart crashed against his rib cage as the scream came again. The sound of sheer terror ripped through him. The minute he entered the dark bedroom, he saw his daughter silhouetted in front of the window.

As he grabbed Melanie and pulled her tight against his chest, Amanda flipped on the overhead light. The sleep glaze in Melanie's eyes fell away and she uttered a single small sob as she wrapped her arms around his neck.

When he realized it must have been the darkness of the room and a bad dream that had tumbled her out of bed and not some physical threat, he relaxed a bit.

"Shh, it's all right," he soothed as he stroked down her trembling back. "It was just a dream, just a very bad dream." Although he said the words, he knew it was a very bad memory that had caused his daughter to scream.

While he held and tried to calm her, Amanda took the night-light out of the wall outlet. He was almost relieved that they had left the office. As he'd sat talking to her, all he'd been able to think about was whether her lips tasted as soft and yielding as they looked, or if her sweet-smelling hair felt like silk.

It was a dangerous train of thought. The last thing he wanted or needed was the complication of a woman in his life. His life was complicated enough as it was. No matter how attractive he found Amanda Rockport, he'd do well to remember he had more important things on his plate…like staying out of prison.

Within minutes Melanie had calmed and been tucked back into bed. Sawyer got a new lightbulb out of her dresser drawer and changed the burnt out one in the night-light.

He remained in the doorway until he was certain Melanie was once again asleep, then he stepped into the hallway where Amanda awaited him.

"The bulb in the night-light needs to be changed once a week, no matter what," he said. In the close confines of the hallway her scent eddied in the air, the bewitching scent of night-blooming jasmine.

"Will she be all right?" she asked, her concern evident in her voice.

"She should be fine for the rest of the night. She

has occasional nightmares. That's why the night-light is so important." He swept a hand through his hair as a deep sorrow cut through him.

Would Melanie forever be scarred by that night? He should have made different choices. Guilt and recriminations ripped him up inside. He should have done things differently, then none of this would have happened.

She took a step toward him. "Children are amazingly resilient, Sawyer." She placed a hand on his forearm, her long slender fingers warm on his arm. "She'll be fine in time."

There was a softness, an innocence about her that he wanted to fall into. Somehow in the past couple of years he'd forgotten about kindness and innocence and the inviting softness that some women possessed.

He stepped back from her, and her hand fell to her side. "The problem is I don't know how much time I have." He motioned her toward the stairs and away from Melanie's bedroom. "I don't know when there's going to be a knock on the door and Lucas Jamison will be standing there with an arrest warrant."

They started down the stairs. "Lucas Jamison? Is he a policeman?" she asked.

"He's a good friend, but he's also the sheriff." They reached the bottom of the stairs. "Would you like a cup of coffee?" he asked. He wasn't ready to call it a night, wasn't prepared for the nightmares his own sleep would probably bring.

"A cup of coffee would be nice," she agreed, and followed him into the kitchen. She sat at the table while he put on half a pot to brew.

When the coffee began to gurgle into the glass carafe he turned back to face her. "What are you doing here?"

A tiny frown danced across her forehead. "What do you mean?"

"I mean why would you leave your home to travel to a small bayou in Louisiana to take a nanny job and work for a man you'd never met? I've seen your credentials. You could have a job anywhere."

"I had a job at a local middle school in Kansas City, but I decided I needed a change." Her gaze didn't quite meet his. He had the feeling that there was more to her story than she was telling.

Even though she was Johnny's younger sister, before hiring her he had done a thorough background check. He knew she had no criminal record, had never been married and, until a couple of months ago, had worked as a counselor at the middle school she'd mentioned.

Her eyes shone as she finally met his gaze. "I'm here to help Melanie, that's all that's important to me. And that should be all that's important to you."

Secrets. Everyone seemed to have a couple. He poured them each a cup of coffee, then joined her at the table. "Melanie likes you," he said.

"I like her." She took a sip of her coffee and studied him above the rim of the cup. She placed her cup back on the table and wrapped her fingers around it. "She seems rather tentative, as if she's anticipating me yelling at her…or hitting her."

Her words created a small ball of rage inside him. He tamped it down and took a drink, then replied, "My wife was a woman who didn't particularly enjoy motherhood. She was often impatient with Melanie." He took another drink to stop himself from speaking ill of the dead.

"It's obvious that Melanie adores you."

"I think that's one of the reasons I'm not in jail at the moment."

She tilted her head and looked at him curiously. "What do you mean?"

"Lucas is aware that Melanie saw something the night of Erica's murder. I think he figures if Melanie saw me kill her mother that night then Melanie would have nothing to do with me now."

"But, that's not necessarily true," she replied. Once again her eyes darkened. "Children often rewrite reality to make it more comfortable, to make it feel safe. Children also have the capacity to create a fantasy and make it real to them."

"Do me a favor, don't mention those kinds of things to Lucas. I have enough problems as it is."

"I can't imagine any reason I'd have to speak to the sheriff." She frowned. "But I'd like to ask you about George."

"What about him?"

Her frown deepened, and her fingers laced and

unlaced in her lap. "He mentioned today that if I wanted to go sightseeing he'd be happy to take me the same places he used to take your wife."

Sawyer sighed, leaned back and raked a hand through his hair. "George is a lot of talk. I know he told Erica about several clubs in town at one time. If he's making you uncomfortable, I'll talk to him."

"That won't be necessary. I don't want any trouble," she said hurriedly. "If there's nothing else? I'm more tired than I realized."

He stood and shook his head. "I'd like a check-in from you each evening after Melanie is in bed. I want to know everything that's going on with her, what happens in the hours while I'm at work."

"Of course," she said, standing. She carried her cup to the sink and rinsed it, then started for the doorway.

"I assumed you read the reports about my wife's murder? Then you must know that she was pregnant at the time of her death." She stopped walking and nodded, her blue eyes shadowing with a touch of sympathy.

"I read the newspaper accounts this morning," she said.

"What the newspaper accounts couldn't tell you was that the baby wasn't mine." Her eyes flared slightly with surprise, but he didn't give her a chance to reply. "I'll see you tomorrow, Amanda."

He released a deep sigh as she disappeared out of the kitchen. He took his cup to the sink and added it to hers, then left the kitchen and returned to his study.

Once there he poured himself a glass of Scotch, then walked over to the wall that held all the pictures. His gaze focused on the picture of Erica. She'd been insanely beautiful and selfish and unfaithful.

He wasn't sure when the affairs had begun. For all he knew she'd started seeing other men soon after their wedding. It didn't matter now. The only thing that mattered was that Melanie had already lost one parent. He didn't want her to lose him.

His gaze moved to the picture of the six men. The Brotherhood, that's what they'd called themselves when they'd arrived at Riverhead College, the prestigious private school in southern Missouri. They had been five young men, best friends, from the wealthiest families in Conja Creek.

In those four years of school, they'd shared kegs of beer, lots of laughs and a solemn promise to have each other's backs.

He stared at the face of Lucas Jamison, Sheriff of Conja Creek. Good friend, fellow member of the Brotherhood, but despite the promise they had all made to each other so many years ago, how long would Lucas be able to overlook the damning circumstantial evidence and keep him out of jail?

THE BABY WASN'T HIS.

The words played and replayed in her mind the next day as she and Melanie set up for a tea party in Melanie's room. As Melanie arranged her stuffed teddy bears into chairs at the miniature table, Amanda unboxed a tiny tea set that probably cost as much as a month's rent on her apartment back home.

The baby wasn't his. That meant that before her death Erica had been having an affair. That knowledge certainly added a nail into the coffin of suspicion where Sawyer was concerned. Everyone probably believed that he'd found out about the baby and killed her in some kind of jealous rage.

But despite the evidence, there was a big part of Amanda that wanted to believe, needed to believe, that he was innocent.

"I see you have Ms. Panda Bear at the head of the table," she now said to Melanie. The black and white bear was slightly bedraggled. "She must be a favorite of yours."

Melanie nodded and smiled at the bear as if it were a beloved sibling, then she gestured Amanda into one of the two empty chairs.

The little teapot was already filled with apple juice, and Helen had promised fresh-baked cookies in fifteen minutes. As Amanda sat at the table, Melanie walked over to the massive wooden toy chest and nearly disappeared into it as she rummaged around. When she stood back up she held two feather boas in her hands.

She walked over to Amanda and placed the bright-pink one around her shoulders, then slung the purple one over her own and giggled with delight.

"I see we're dressing for tea."

The voice came from the doorway, and Amanda

whirled around to see Lillian standing there. "Lillian!" she exclaimed in surprise, wondering how the woman had not only gotten inside the house but had climbed the stairs without being heard.

"Looks like fun," she said.

"Would you like to join us?" Amanda asked.

Lillian smiled. "No, but I have a message to deliver from Helen." She looked at Melanie. "Helen says if you come to the kitchen the cookies are ready and there's a bowl of frosting that needs to be licked."

Melanie's face lit up as she looked at Amanda. Amanda stood and pulled the boa from around her neck. "Go on," she said. "We can have our tea party later."

The words were scarcely out of her mouth before Melanie disappeared from the room. Lillian laughed. "She's a doll, isn't she?"

"She seems very sweet and easy to get along with," Amanda agreed.

"But troubled." Lillian's smooth smile fell away, and she moved to the window to stare outside. "I wish we all knew what she'd seen the night that Erica was murdered. I wish we could take that vision out of her head and see the guilty person behind bars."

"Do you know who Erica was having an affair with?" Amanda asked.

Lillian turned from the window to look at her. "So…Sawyer told you she was unfaithful?"

"He told me that the baby she was carrying at the time of her death wasn't his."

Moving away from the window, Lillian sighed. "Erica was my best friend, but she loved keeping secrets. She was beautiful and full of life, but she was also the most selfish, indulgent, amoral woman I've ever known." Tears filled her eyes. "She could also be generous and fun loving, and I miss her so much it's terrible." She blinked back the tears and drew a deep breath. "And no, I have no idea who Erica might have been sleeping with at the time of her death."

"Isn't it possible that it was her lover who killed her?" Amanda asked. She didn't want to upset Lillian, but it was possible she might unconsciously hold a clue.

"I'm sure Lucas is looking at that angle," Lillian replied. "So, less than forty-eight hours in the house and Sawyer has already convinced you of his innocence?"

"You don't think he's innocent?" Amanda asked.

"I adore Sawyer. I think he's a good man, but even a good man could have been pushed to extremes by Erica." She laughed drily. "There were times I wanted to throttle her." Her laugh strangled in her throat as tears once again filled her eyes.

Amanda wasn't sure how to respond and thankfully at that time Melanie reappeared in the doorway, a platter of freshly baked cookies in her hands.

"Ah, I see the tea party is about to begin," Lillian said. "You two go ahead. I just stopped by to see how you were getting along."

Amanda walked with her to the bedroom door. "We're doing fine."

Lillian placed a hand on Amanda's forearm. "Why don't we do lunch on Saturday? I'd love to show you around, and I imagine Sawyer is planning on being home for the day."

"He hasn't told me his plans for the weekend," Amanda replied. "He mentioned I should have weekends off. If that's the case, I'd like to have lunch." It would be nice to have a woman friend, somebody she could talk to, perhaps confide in. It would also be nice to see a little bit of the town whose name implied bewitchment.

"Great, I'll call you and we can firm up the plans." She smiled at Melanie. "Aunt Lilly will see you later, okay, sweetheart?"

Melanie nodded, and with a wave of her fingers, Lillian left the room.

The tea party was a success, but as Amanda played pretend with Melanie she couldn't help but think about what little Lillian had told her. Erica had been sleeping with somebody at the time of her death, somebody who had gotten her pregnant. Was it possible that that somebody had killed Erica so that the secret affair would never see the light of day?

Sawyer was home in time for dinner, and as they shared the evening meal Amanda mentioned to him Lillian's visit and the question about the weekend plans.

"I'll be home all day Saturday so you're free to

take off and have lunch with Lillian or whatever," he said. He was still dressed in his business clothes and looked unbelievably attractive. He'd shucked his suit jacket and had his white shirtsleeves rolled up to expose his muscled forearms.

He smiled at his daughter. "I'm sure we can find something to occupy ourselves, right, sweetie?" Melanie nodded and gazed at her father with adoring eyes.

Could she have seen her father stab her mother to death, then shove her into the murky swamp water and still look at him as if he hung the moon?

Amanda reminded herself that it wasn't her place to discern whether Sawyer Bennett was guilty or not. Her job was to take care of Melanie. Nothing more, nothing less.

Melanie had just been excused from the table to go upstairs to her room when a knock sounded at the door. A moment later Helen ushered in a tall, dark-haired man wearing the brown uniform of the local sheriff.

"Lucas," Sawyer said and stood.

"Evening, Sawyer." He looked curiously at Amanda.

"This is Amanda Rockport, my new nanny," Sawyer replied.

"Sorry to intrude," Lucas said. He directed his focus back to Sawyer. "We need to talk."

"So talk," Sawyer replied and sat back down. He gestured to the chair Melanie had vacated.

"You might want to discuss this in private." Lucas shifted from foot to foot.

"If this has something to do with Erica's murder investigation, then I have nothing to hide from Amanda. If you don't need the privacy, then I don't. Take a load off, Lucas, and tell me why you're here."

Amanda watched as Lucas folded his long body into the chair. The tension between the two men was palpable in the air, and Amanda didn't know whether she should excuse herself or not.

"I've got pressure, Sawyer, pressure to make an arrest," Lucas said.

"Then find the person responsible and do it," Sawyer replied smoothly.

Lucas rubbed the center of his forehead with two fingers, as if fighting a headache. "I'm doing my best, but I've got no other viable suspects, nothing to go on and all fingers pointing at you."

"Then arrest me." Sawyer's voice was deep, filled with suppressed emotion.

A knot of apprehension twisted in Amanda's stomach, a knot formed by more than a little bit of selfish need. She didn't want Sawyer arrested. If that happened she'd be out of a job and she didn't want to go through the process of finding another one. Besides, even though it had only been two days, she'd grown incredibly attached to Melanie.

"Ah, hell, Sawyer, I've known you all my life. I know you aren't a killer." Lucas dropped his hand from his forehead, his dark eyes pained. "But I just wanted to let you know that the pressure is on and I don't know how much longer I'm going to be able to stop the inevitable."

Sawyer held his friend's gaze for a long moment. "I don't want you to jeopardize your position because of friendship."

"I'll try to buy you some more time, but I thought you should know that unless we can find a decent lead to follow or a person of interest to investigate, the mayor and the DA are going to push for your arrest." He stood and Sawyer rose, as well.

"I'll see you out."

As Sawyer and the sheriff left the dining room, Amanda tried to still the beating of her heart. So, the noose was tightening around Sawyer.

If he went to jail, she supposed Lillian and James would take Melanie, and Amanda would be forced to return to Kansas City.

And what will you do there? a little voice whispered in her head. Fall back into the dark depression that you suffered before you took this job? She thought of the reason she'd been forced to resign from the job she had loved, remembered all the people who had distanced themselves from her, people she'd thought had been her friends.

She couldn't go back there. She'd have to start all over someplace else. She was jolted out of her self-absorbed pity party as she thought of Melanie.

She'd lost her mother, and if Sawyer were arrested she would lose her father. No matter how close the child felt to the Cordells, it wouldn't be the same as having a parent to raise her.

Amanda's heart ached for her. She knew what it was like to grow up without parents. An aunt and uncle had raised her and Johnny when their parents had died in a car accident. As loving as her aunt and uncle had been, it hadn't been the same as being raised by loving parents.

Melanie needed her daddy, more than ever now, and Amanda needed this job. She was pulled from her thoughts as Sawyer returned to the living room.

While Lucas had been present, Sawyer had appeared relaxed, but now his lips were nothing more than a thin slash in a face taut with strain.

He sat in his chair and looked at her, his dark green eyes empty and hollow. "Time is running out for me. Eventually Lucas will have to make an arrest, and I'm the only suspect around. I've got to find out who Erica was having an affair with before her death, because my gut tells me that's who murdered her."

"Can I do anything to help?"

His features relaxed a bit and he looked at her thoughtfully. "Maybe. Tonight after Melanie goes to bed I'm going to search Erica's room again and see if I can find anything that might give me some answers. Maybe you'll see something that I missed before, something that the authorities didn't notice when they searched."

"Sure, I'll help you look," she agreed.

"Come to my office after Melanie is asleep and we'll get started then." Some of the stress lines smoothed out as he stood once again. "And now I'm going to find my daughter and play a game with her. I'd better spend every moment possible with her in case…" He frowned and allowed his words to fall away, then left the dining room.

Amanda grabbed her napkin from her lap and placed it on the table next to her plate, her heart throbbing with anxiety. What on earth had she stepped into? And why, despite all the evidence to the contrary did her heart tell her that Sawyer wasn't guilty?

She could only hope that she and Sawyer found something tonight in the dead woman's belongings, something that pointed to the real guilty party.

Chapter Four

Melanie was asleep by eight-thirty. By the illumination of the night-light Amanda could see the
slight puff of her little lips with each exhale. She
fought the impulse to lean over and swipe a strand
of the little girl's hair away from her cheek.

She was falling in love with Melanie. In the two
days she'd been with her, the little girl had managed
to crawl into Amanda's heart like no other child
had ever done before.

Maybe it was because Melanie was so needy,
locked inside herself by a terrible trauma. Or perhaps it was the fact that somehow, deep inside,
Amanda thought that if she could help Melanie, if
she could save Melanie, it would take away the
memory of Bobby Miller.

She shoved the painful thoughts of Bobby aside
and left Melanie's room. As she walked down the
massive staircase, she found herself wondering why
Sawyer didn't have more household help. Certainly

he could afford it. Helen and George were the only two people she'd seen, but she knew the house and the estate were too large for two people to care for.

And what about Melanie's friends? Didn't she have schoolmates who she might like to see? Little friends who not only might manage to make her giggle, but also might prompt her to talk? She made a note to herself to ask Sawyer about Melanie's friends.

Now that Melanie was asleep, it was time for her to meet Sawyer in his office, time for them to go through a dead woman's things to try to find some hint of who might be responsible for her murder.

She found Sawyer seated at his desk, the faint scent of good Scotch lingering in the air. He held up a glass. "Would you like one?"

She shook her head. "No, thanks, I'm not much of a drinker."

He stared at the amber liquid. "I wasn't until Erica's death." He drained the glass, then stood. "I realize I'm asking you to do something that has nothing to do with the duties I hired you for."

She preceded him out of the office and headed for the stairs. "I don't mind. I understand how important this is."

"It's not just my life we're talking about, but it's Melanie's, as well." His voice radiated suppressed emotion, and Amanda was grateful he was behind her and she couldn't see the pain she knew darkened his eyes.

She had absolutely no reason to trust this man,

no concrete reason to believe in his innocence, except the fact that she believed, in her heart, in her soul, that he had not committed the crime. Maybe she was crazy to be so sure. She certainly felt no fear of him, nothing to make her wary.

Still, the situation was heartbreaking. A man facing murder charges and a little girl at risk of losing the only parent she had left. Somehow the fact that Amanda would be without a job if Sawyer went to jail paled in comparison to the price Melanie would pay.

When she reached the top of the stairs, she stopped and let Sawyer take the lead. He didn't take her to the end of the hall where she knew the master suite was, but rather opened the bedroom door that had been closed since Amanda had arrived at the house.

"Erica didn't share my bedroom," he said, and ushered her into a room that was a pink riot of ruffles and lace. Clothes were strewn everywhere and makeup and jewelry cluttered the top of a vanity dresser. "As you can see, she wasn't into housekeeping, and the sheriff and his men weren't exactly neat when they searched. I haven't had anything done in here since…" His voice trailed off.

Erica wasn't "into" housekeeping. She wasn't into mothering and obviously she wasn't into being faithful. Erica couldn't be more alien to Amanda. She looked at Sawyer, wondering what was going through his mind as he looked at the bed where his wife had slept and the clothes she'd worn before her death.

His features were a stoic mask, giving nothing away of his internal thoughts. "The authorities searched here immediately after Erica was found, but they found nothing they thought might be important to the case." The mask slipped slightly, and a fire of anger shone from his eyes. "I think most of the investigators had already come to the mistaken conclusion that I was their man."

"Then let's find something that proves them wrong," she replied.

The anger in his eyes faded and a hint of gratitude took its place. "Why don't I start in the closet and you can go through the drawers."

"Sounds like a plan," she agreed.

As he disappeared into the walk-in closet, she went to the dresser and pulled out the top drawer. It contained panties and bras, little wisps of colorful material that Amanda couldn't imagine fitting a grown woman. It somehow felt obscene, digging into items that had belonged to another woman, a woman who was no longer among the living.

If Amanda died and anyone went through her underwear drawer, all they would find would be white cotton underpants and sturdy, no-nonsense bras.

For about a half an hour, she and Sawyer worked in silence. The sound of him pulling things off shelves and opening boxes drifted from the closet, but other than that he didn't make a sound.

The dresser yielded nothing but clothes. She took each drawer out and checked beneath to make sure there was nothing hidden on the bottom or inside the dresser.

When she was finished with the dresser, she moved to the vanity. Makeup, hand and body lotions and perfumes filled the two drawers. A jewelry box spilled its contents over the top of the vanity. Sparkling bracelets and necklaces competed with cocktail rings and shiny earrings. But there was nothing there to point a finger at a killer.

By the time she'd gone through those drawers, Sawyer stepped out of the closet, an expression of defeat on his handsome features.

"Nothing. I didn't find anything that might be helpful." He sat on the edge of the bed.

Amanda remained seated on the vanity stool. "I didn't find anything, either. Is there anyplace else we could look? Anyplace else in the house where she might have kept private things?"

He leaned forward and covered his face with his hands, his shoulders slumped in obvious defeat. "I don't know." He straightened up and dropped his hands to his side. "It seems I knew less about the woman I was married to than I thought I did." He looked around the room, then gazed back at Amanda.

"I was going to divorce her. I'd finally made up my mind. I'd stayed for Melanie's sake but had come to the conclusion that Melanie would be better off coming from a broken home, rather than living in one. Then Erica was murdered."

"You didn't love her anymore?" Amanda asked.

There was something contemplative in his expression, something that made her think he needed to talk.

He smiled wryly. "I'm not sure I ever truly loved Erica. It was definitely lust at first sight, and she fascinated me. She was unlike any woman I'd ever known before. She was unpredictable and passionate about life. She got pregnant with Melanie almost immediately and we got married."

He looked around the room, then back at her. "Deep inside, I knew we'd made a mistake, that we had different ideas about marriage, about love. But then Melanie came and I hoped Erica would finally settle down." He sighed. "I was wrong. What about you? Left some broken hearts in your path?"

She smiled and shook her head. "I'm certainly not the kind of woman to leave broken hearts behind."

He tilted his head, his gaze intent as it lingered on her. "Now, why would you say something like that about yourself?"

She laughed self-consciously. "I'm not particularly fascinating. I don't stir great passion in anyone." She averted her gaze and tried not to think about the one person she'd apparently stirred something in, a young boy who had wound up dead.

"On the contrary," Sawyer said, and she looked back at him. "I find several things about you quite fascinating."

The air in the room seemed to thin, making it more difficult for her to catch her breath. "Like what?" she managed to ask.

He stood, walked over to her and held out his hand. "Let's get out of here. This room reeks of unhappiness."

She placed her hand in his and allowed him to pull her out into the hallway. He dropped her hand when they reached the stairs, and she followed him down and into the living room.

He opened the French doors that led out to the patio. "How about we step outside and get a breath of fresh air?"

She followed him outside where the sultry night air closed in around them and the scent of flowers mingled with the underlying odor of thick vegetation.

Insects buzzed and clicked from the swamp and occasionally a ripple sounded from the water as some creature entered or exited the murky depths.

He stood close enough to her that she could smell him, a hint of minty soap and a spicy cologne. "Erica was wild and crazy and many men found her fascinating. But I find your calm composure intriguing. I find your gentleness with my daughter charming."

Once again the air seemed to be too insubstantial to fill her lungs. Was he trying to charm her? To manipulate her so she'd be on his side in the mess that had become his life?

He took several steps away from her and stared up at the moon that hung low and plump in the sky. "Johnny used to talk about you a lot in college, his little sister who seemed to have her life more together than he ever hoped to have."

She smiled, her heart swelling as she thought of her brother. "Johnny can't seem to find his place in life."

"And you've found yours?" His green eyes glittered in the moonlight.

"I thought I had." He waited, as if expecting her to go on, but she couldn't tell him what had thrown her off track, what tragic event had reshaped her life. She wasn't ready to talk about that. "Life has a way of throwing curveballs that sometimes make you change your path."

He laughed without humor. "Tell me about it."

"What made you and your friends choose a college in Missouri to attend?" she asked, wanting a change in the subject.

"Riverhead College is a prestigious private school. At the time, my friends and I wanted to get out of Conja Creek, away from the swamps and our parents, and we decided to go there."

"The Brotherhood," she said softly. "Johnny was thrilled when you all accepted him into your fold. He was there on a working scholarship and was convinced he'd be miserable, but you guys made his college experience some of the best years of his life."

His smile softened his features and made him impossibly handsome. "They were some of the best years for all of us, and Johnny is a terrific guy."

"You're an architect and I know Lucas is the sheriff. What happened to the other members of the Brotherhood?" she asked curiously.

"Jackson Burdeaux is a successful defense attorney who has offices both here in town and in Baton Rouge. Clay Jefferson is a psychiatrist and I've lost track of Beau. He left town a couple years ago and nobody has heard from him since."

She knew what he was doing…talking about anything and everything except the fact that the sheriff had told him he was running out of time.

"What are you going to do now?" she asked softly.

Once again he stared up at the moon, as if seeking answers that would make sense of everything. He sighed, then looked at her. "Up until now I placed my trust, my faith in Lucas. I felt confident that he'd be able to find out who was responsible for Erica's death. He's a smart man, a good sheriff, and I just assumed he'd solve this crime without any problems."

"But that's not happened."

"I know. And I think if I'm going to stay out of jail it's time I do a little sleuthing on my own."

She frowned at him curiously. "What do you mean?"

"I need to go where Erica went, to the clubs where she hung out. I need to meet the people she knew, people who might know who she was sleeping with at the time of her death." His eyes narrowed slightly. "Why don't you come with me? Maybe people would be more apt to talk to you than to me. We could go Saturday night. I'll get Lillian to sit with Melanie."

There was a part of her that knew she was getting in too deep, going places she'd never imagined she'd go when she'd taken this job. But the appeal on his face was intense, and she found herself nodding her assent.

In the distance a thrashing in the water followed a small-animal scream. Amanda shivered and wondered what exactly she'd gotten herself into.

SATURDAY MORNING Amanda, Sawyer and Melanie were seated at breakfast when the doorbell rang. A moment later Helen ushered in a tall, husky blond man Sawyer introduced as Adam Kincaid, his business partner.

"Ah, the lovely Amanda," Adam exclaimed, his blue eyes twinkling with a charming flirtatiousness. "Sawyer has been singing your praises since the day you started working."

"Sit down, Adam, and don't overwork that Southern charm of yours," Sawyer said drily.

"Ah, but working my charm is what I do best," he replied, and winked at Amanda. He sat in the chair next to Melanie and leaned over and pretended to pull a quarter from her ear.

Melanie took the quarter with a smile, then looked expectantly at her father. "Yes, you can be excused," he said.

With another smile directed at Amanda, she flew from the room. Sawyer had told his daughter that as soon as she cleaned her room, he'd take her into town to buy her something special.

Officially it was Amanda's day off, and Lillian

was picking her up to take her to lunch. Then this evening she and Sawyer were going out to see if they could discover anything about who Erica might have been seeing at the time of her death.

Adam reached forward and grabbed one of the biscuits from the platter. "Nobody makes biscuits like Helen." He broke it in two and grabbed Sawyer's knife to spread some butter.

"You'll have to excuse my partner," Sawyer said. "He often shows up on Saturday mornings to mooch breakfast."

At that moment Helen came through the door carrying a plate of bacon and eggs and a cup of coffee. She placed them in front of Adam, who smiled up at her. "Ah, the lovely Helen. You light up my morning with your smile."

She scowled at him. "And you are as full of it as you ever were."

"You wound me," Adam exclaimed.

She sniffed indignantly and left the room.

"Of all the household help you kept, I'll never understand why you decided to keep that sour woman," Adam observed.

"Because she's the only help who was loyal to me, the only one who stayed after Erica's death," Sawyer replied. "Besides, she adores Melanie, and Melanie loves her."

Amanda digested this information. It went a long way in explaining why there were no other people working in the house. Apparently, most of them had left when Erica had been murdered. She'd asked Sawyer about Melanie's school friends earlier that morning, and he'd told her that he'd intentionally kept his daughter isolated since her mother's death, afraid of the gossip she might hear if she went visiting at any of her friends' homes.

Adam looked at Amanda. "I guess you know what's happened with Erica and everything. Hell of a mess our boy here has found himself in." He turned his attention back to Sawyer. "Just say the word. I'll buy you out and you can leave the country."

Sawyer raised one of his dark eyebrows. "And why would I want to do that? I'm innocent."

"Lots of innocent men have spent a lifetime behind bars," Adam replied.

"Thanks for reminding me," Sawyer replied.

"I just want you to be prepared for anything the future might bring," Adam said. He turned his attention to Amanda and for the next few minutes he asked her questions about where she'd come from and how she liked Louisiana.

When the talk turned to their latest building project, Amanda excused herself and went up to find Melanie. Amanda stood in the doorway between the two rooms and watched Melanie put her toys in the toy chest.

"You're doing a terrific job," she said. "Your daddy will be proud of how clean you've made your room."

Melanie smiled and continued finishing up as Amanda got ready for her lunch date with Lillian.

She was looking forward to some girl chat, something to keep her mind off the night ahead.

Tonight she and Sawyer were leaving the house at nine to explore Erica's world. In the three days since they'd searched Erica's room, they had fallen into the routine of spending the evenings together.

After Melanie fell asleep, Amanda would join him either at the kitchen table or on the patio for a cup of coffee or a glass of wine. Once they'd walked out to the dock where Sawyer seemed to draw strength from the wildness of the surroundings.

During those late evenings, they'd talked about everything…except Erica's murder and the reason Amanda had resigned from her previous job.

Each and every moment she spent in his presence heightened the simmering tension she felt inside, a tension she recognized as sexual. But more than that, she found herself drawn to him on levels that had nothing to do with desire.

She perceived a core sense of loneliness inside him, one that spoke to a similar emotion in her. She'd been lonely for most of her life and she had the feeling that, despite his marriage, he'd been lonely, as well.

She had to keep reminding herself that he was a man whose life was in turmoil and that there was no place for her in it other than as his daughter's nanny. But there had been several times in the past week when it would have been easy to forget that fact, when his gaze had lingered on her longer than necessary, when she'd felt a need radiating from him that she wanted to fill.

Sawyer and Melanie left for their trip into town around eleven and at noon Lillian arrived to pick up Amanda. Within minutes the two were in her car heading for the downtown area of Conja Creek.

"I guess there's been no change with Melanie? She still isn't talking?" Lillian asked as she maneuvered the narrow road.

"No, no change." Amanda fought a wave of depression, then reminded herself that time was the only thing that would heal Melanie. "She's a sweetheart even if she isn't talking. I put up a dry-erase board in her room so she's communicating some by writing on it."

"She's a little doll. I'm not sure Erica realized just how lucky she was."

"Sawyer told me he was going to divorce her," Amanda said.

Lillian sighed. "I'm not surprised. If he had, Erica probably would have made his life a living hell."

As they entered the quaint town of Conja Creek, Lillian began to point out various stores she liked and didn't like. "There's Linda's Hair and Nails. Stay away from there. Linda likes to do things her way and she has an odd sense of style. Go to the Curl Boutique. It's down the street."

By the time they reached the Bayou Kitchen, the restaurant where they would be having lunch, Amanda knew where to buy her clothes, the best places to eat and where to go to purchase the latest fashions in shoes.

"It's not New York, but there's enough old money here that the shops are higher quality than most Southern small towns." Lillian pulled into the parking space in front of the restaurant and shut off the engine. "This is my favorite place to eat around here. Most of the items on the menu are *so* not on my diet, but I indulge at least once a week."

Amanda smiled. There wasn't a spare ounce of flesh on Lillian's body. However, Amanda always had ten pounds she was trying to take off. But once they were seated at the table inside, she decided to throw caution to the wind and ordered a platter of deep-fried shrimp and fries. Lillian ordered shrimp scampi, and as they ate she talked about the people of Conja Creek.

"Old money, that's what built Conja Creek. There were a dozen families who were the founders, each one wealthier than the other. Sawyer and his high-school buddies all came from those families, but you'd never know it. From what Erica told me, in college those guys all agreed to work at giving back to society or some such nonsense."

"I find that admirable," Amanda replied.

Lillian smiled. "Well, of course it is, but it sure aggravated Erica. She used to complain that, other than the house where they lived, Sawyer didn't act like he was wealthy. I think she married him with visions of trips to Europe and shopping sprees in Paris."

"From what I've seen in her bedroom, Sawyer was very generous." Amanda picked up one of the last of her shrimp. When she looked at Lillian once again the woman was staring at her with a look of speculation. "What? What's wrong."

"Amanda, you seem like a nice woman. I'd hate to see you get involved on any kind of personal level with Sawyer. He's a man who has just lost his wife, a man on the rebound, and you're a pretty little convenience."

The warmth of a blush swept over Amanda's face. "I have no intention of getting involved with Sawyer. I'm his daughter's nanny, nothing more."

Lillian stabbed a shrimp with her fork. "I just don't want to see you get hurt. As far as I'm concerned the only thing worse than death is falling in love with the wrong man."

"Been there, done that," Amanda replied, her thoughts drifting back in time to the man she'd thought had loved her, but who had run at the first sign of trouble. It didn't hurt anymore to think about Scott, and that made her wonder just how deep her love for him had been.

"What's this I hear about you and Sawyer going out tonight to try to find out something about Erica? He's bringing Melanie to my house at eight to spend the night and told me you and he were going to go hunting for her lover."

"That's the plan," Amanda said, and her heart quickened slightly. She told herself it had nothing to do with the thought of spending the evening alone in Sawyer's company. Surely her racing heart had to do with the fact that they were seeking a murderer.

Chapter Five

As Sawyer drove away from James and Lillian's place where he'd just left Melanie for the night, his thoughts turned to the night ahead.

With every hour that passed he was aware of a clock ticking off the minutes of his freedom. Lucas would only be able to stall so long and unless Sawyer found another reasonable suspect, he was going to be arrested.

He frowned and tightened his hands on the steering wheel. When Erica had insisted they name James and Lillian as godparents to Melanie, Sawyer had never imagined there being a time when they would be raising his daughter.

But there was no other choice. Both his parents and Erica's were dead. There were no aunts or uncles, no other family members to take in Melanie. He'd certainly rather see her with James and Lillian than in the foster care system. Of course the best-case scenario would be that the guilty party was identified and Sawyer and his daughter picked up the pieces of their lives and remained together.

He pulled up in front of his house, and his thoughts turned to Amanda. Other than Melanie, Amanda had become a point of light in the darkness that had become his life.

He'd found comfort in the mundane conversations they shared over meals, in the easy relationship she was building with Melanie. He enjoyed her company and the fact that, despite all the evidence to the contrary, she seemed to believe in his innocence. He needed somebody on his side in this mess.

There were moments in the evenings when he felt Amanda's gaze lingering on him, when he became aware of a tension between them, a tension that wasn't altogether unpleasant.

He cut the engine but remained in the car, staring at the house where he'd once thought he'd build his family, share happiness and fulfill dreams.

The dreams had shattered and there had never been much happiness within those walls. Maybe it was time to call Jackson Burdeaux, his old college buddy and fellow member of the Brotherhood. Maybe he should have been in touch with the defense attorney all along.

He'd been functioning in a fog since Erica's murder, and it was only in the past week or two that the fog had lifted and the reality of his situation had struck him. He couldn't depend on Lucas to fix things. And he had to be prepared for the worst.

As he climbed out of the car he made a mental note to call Jackson first thing Monday morning. He'd been a fool not to have done it the moment Erica's body had been found. He'd been a fool about a lot of things.

And tonight he and Amanda would delve into Erica's world and see if they could discover who might have had a motive to kill her.

He entered the house and went directly to his office to wait for Amanda. He'd told her they would leave around nine. Erica's world had never started early in the evening.

He'd just sat behind his desk when Helen appeared in the doorway. "I'm leaving now," she said. "There's a roast in the refrigerator for tomorrow. All you'll need to do is warm it up." Sundays were Helen's day off and she usually prepared something that could easily be reheated for that day.

"Thanks, Helen," he replied. She nodded and turned to leave but stopped as he called her name once again. "Helen, I don't think I've ever told you how much I appreciate you sticking with us."

She offered him a tight smile. "You don't have to thank me. You should know I'd do anything for Melanie," she replied. "Good night." After she'd left the office, Sawyer leaned back in his chair, closed his eyes and rubbed a hand wearily across his forehead.

"You don't look like a man who's ready to kick up your heels in town."

He opened his eyes to see Amanda standing in

the doorway, and his breath half caught in his throat. He'd seen her every day for the past week, but he'd never seen her looking like she did at that moment.

Black jeans hugged her legs, and a turquoise knit blouse emphasized the thrust of her breasts and the blue of her eyes. Black-and-turquoise earrings dangled from her ears and her makeup wasn't as subtle as usual.

As far as he was concerned she'd looked like a nanny before, but now she looked like a hot young woman ready to go out on the town. His gaze lingered on her lips, sweetly curved and glossed with a soft pink.

Her fingers curled against the sides of her jeans and she frowned. "Am I underdressed?" she asked, obviously self-conscious beneath his intent gaze.

"No, not at all. You're perfect." His pulse had accelerated at the sight of her and it seemed to have no intention of returning to normal. "Are we ready?"

Minutes later they were in his car and headed into town. "Will Melanie be okay with Lillian and James for the night?" she asked.

"Yeah, she'll be fine. Even when Erica was alive, Melanie would occasionally spend the night with them."

"They don't have children of their own?"

"No. They never had any children. They're nice people, but they've become accustomed to living their lives without kids. Lillian adores Melanie, but I can't imagine her being a full-time mother."

He could smell Amanda, a soft, evocative scent that didn't scream into a man's senses, but rather whispered through them. It was at that moment that he recognized he wanted her. It was a desire that had been building with each day that passed, with each moment he spent in her company. And it was one he had no intention of following through on.

Only a selfish man would begin an affair with a woman knowing that at any moment he might go to prison for the rest of his life. And Sawyer didn't see himself as a selfish man. At the moment he was simply a desperate one, desperate to find out who his wife had been sleeping with, who might have had a motive for murdering her.

"Our first stop is Cajun Country," he said. "It's kind of a rough bar on the edge of town. George told me it was one of Erica's favorite places."

"I don't understand why a woman who had all the things Erica had would want to go out and take the kind of chances she did. I mean, she had you and Melanie and a beautiful home. She had everything most women dream of having."

He remained silent for a few minutes, thoughts of his wife flitting through his head. "According to Lillian, Erica had a difficult childhood. Erica refused to talk about her past when we got married, so I don't know too much about her family life. All I know is that she seemed to have a hole inside her that she was constantly trying to fill. I couldn't fill it. Melanie couldn't. I'm not sure that anything or anyone could have."

"That's tragic," Amanda said softly.

"I asked her dozens of times to get some counseling. You know that one of my college buddies, Clay Jefferson, is a psychiatrist. But she refused."

"Then, there was nothing more you could have done," she replied.

"I just wish now I had been more persuasive about her getting help." He cleared his throat. "How's Melanie? Do you see any cracks in her, any hint that she might be getting better?" he asked. "Any hint that she might talk?"

She cast him a sympathetic smile. "It just doesn't work that way, Sawyer. I can't take her temperature and tell you she's getting better. I can't look into her eyes and know when she might be ready to speak. The only thing I can tell you is that she seems to trust me, that we're getting closer and closer with each day that passes."

"I'm glad." A burst of warmth swept through him that had nothing to do with sexual desire. He wanted his daughter to have somebody she trusted, somebody she could depend on, someone who hadn't been around when her mother had been murdered.

They were quiet for the remainder of the drive. Minutes later he turned off the road and into a driveway that led to their first stop.

Cajun Country was housed in a low, tin-roofed building in the middle of nowhere. The parking area was filled with cars as Sawyer turned in. His stomach clenched as he thought of what lay ahead.

Even through the closed car windows the sound of raucous music was audible. It sounded traditionally Cajun, with pumping accordions, rousing fiddles and the clang of triangles keeping time. It would be a wild crowd, high on booze, the music and life itself. It could also be a dangerous crowd, with volatile emotions that might transform from gaiety to rage in the blink of an eye.

"This is a mistake," he said as his gaze returned to Amanda. "I shouldn't have brought you here."

"Nonsense," she replied crisply. "In fact, I suggest you let me talk. It's possible people will be more open talking to me than they are talking to you." She opened her car door. "We're here, Sawyer, let's see what we can find out."

Reluctantly he got out of the car, and together they walked toward the entrance. The air smelled of boiled crawfish and strong beer, and the sounds of laughter mingled with the music.

As they walked through the door into the dim, smoky interior, he took Amanda's elbow, wanting to claim her as his own to any other men as they entered.

The small dance floor was packed with people. Sawyer held on to Amanda as he angled them through the crowd toward two empty stools at the bar. As they walked he was aware of several male gazes lingering on Amanda, and he tightened his grip on her elbow.

They slid onto the stools and the bartender looked at them expectantly. Sawyer ordered them each a beer, then whirled around on his stool to peruse the crowd. He didn't see anyone he recognized, but that didn't mean some of the people here didn't recognize him.

How many of the men in this place had known Erica? Had they all danced with her, shared drinks with her? As a husband he didn't care anymore who she might have been with. As a murder suspect he definitely cared.

Was there an answer here? Did somebody here know who Erica might have been sleeping with at the time of her death? And had that person killed her?

AMANDA LOOKED AROUND with interest. This place was as alien to her as a monastery in Tibet might have been. The music was foreign, but made it almost impossible for feet to stay still. The dancers looked uninhibited, heads thrown back, feet stomping and hips gyrating.

She sipped the icy beer and shot Sawyer a surreptitious glance. He looked hot, clad in a pair of jeans and a navy T-shirt that hugged his broad shoulders and taut, lean stomach.

She stared back at the dance floor and wondered what it might be like to be held in his strong arms, what it would be like to taste those lips of his that curved so easily into a smile, then pressed so tightly together when he was upset.

Lillian's words came rushing back to her. He had

just lost his wife. He was a man on the rebound, a lonely man, and Amanda would be nothing more than an easy convenience.

For a moment as they'd walked through the door and his hand had been so warm on her elbow, it would have been easy for her to imagine that they were on a date. But this wasn't a date. They were here for a purpose.

With this thought in mind she twirled back around to face the bar and motioned for the bartender. She offered him her most flirtatious smile. "I was wondering if maybe you knew a friend of mine, Erica Bennett?"

The smile on his broad face instantly fell away and his dark brows pulled together in a frown. "I knew her. She's dead." His gaze flicked to Sawyer, who got up from the stool and ambled off to stand nearby. Amanda knew he was distancing himself in hopes the bartender would be more forthcoming with information.

"I know, but she loved coming in here," Amanda said to the bartender. "She told me once that this was one of her favorite places on earth."

The bartender's smile returned and he nodded. "That Erica, she was some kind of crazy. Whenever she came in, the music seemed louder and the fun more intense."

"I'm trying to find out what happened to her, who might have wanted to harm her," Amanda said.

His gaze flickered to Sawyer, then back to her.

"You don't believe he did it? Men have killed their wives for far less in this part of the country."

"Somebody else killed her," Amanda said with assurance. "Can you tell me if she was seeing anyone? If there was a particular man she came in with or spent time with when she was here?"

"She stopped coming in a couple of months before she was killed. I figured maybe she'd left crazy behind and had decided to settle down."

Amanda tried to hide her disappointment at this news. If Erica hadn't been coming here on the nights she left her daughter and her husband, then where had she gone and with whom? Somebody somewhere had to have seen Erica with her lover.

"So you never saw her with any particular man while she was here?" she asked one last time.

He grabbed a wet cloth and wiped down the area in front of her. "Look, I don't want no trouble. I serve drinks and get a paycheck."

"But you also have eyes and you must have seen something," she pressed. "And we're not looking for trouble, either. We're just looking for some answers. Please."

He gave the bar in front of her a final swipe. "The only person I ever saw Erica go off with was the sheriff. Twice he came in and she left with him."

Amanda's heart seemed to stop beating for a moment. "The sheriff? You mean Sheriff Lucas Jamison?"

"That's right. A couple of times they left out of

here together. I figured maybe her husband had gotten the law to bring her home."

Amanda glanced over to where Sawyer stood, his beer in his hand. Lucas Jamison? He was not only the sheriff of Conja Creek, but also one of the Brotherhood, a close friend of Sawyer's.

Had Lucas betrayed his friend? It was frightening to think that the man who might arrest Sawyer might be the real guilty party.

Don't jump to conclusions, she warned herself. As the bartender moved to the opposite end of the bar to wait on somebody else, Sawyer returned to her side.

He leaned close to her, his mouth next to her ear. "Did you learn anything?"

She didn't want to tell him here and now. She had no idea how he might react to the news that his wife had been seen leaving this place a couple of times in the company of the sheriff.

"Let's get out of here," she suggested, and slid off the stool.

Once again he grabbed her elbow, steering her through the crowd and toward the door. She was acutely conscious of the warmth of his touch, the nearness of his body to hers as they headed for the exit. Despite the ripe seafood odor to the air she could smell Sawyer, his clean, masculine scent that had become so familiar to her.

As they walked out into the balmy night air, Amanda tried to figure out how to tell Sawyer what she'd learned.

When they were in the car he turned to look at her. "Did you get any useful information?"

"The bartender said that a couple of months before her death Erica stopped coming in," she replied.

Sawyer stared through the car window toward the bar. "If she wasn't coming here on the nights she left the house, then where was she going?"

"Are there other bars or clubs she might have gone to?"

"There are a couple, but when I talked to George he told me this was Erica's place, that she didn't like any of the other bars."

"You want to try the others? See if we find out anything else?" She didn't want to tell him about Lucas until they were back at the house.

He sighed and rubbed a hand across his forehead, as if his weariness was too great to bear. "Let's just go home. This was probably a stupid idea."

He started the engine and pulled out of the lot and onto the narrow road that would take them back to his house. They didn't speak, the silence in the car growing to stifling proportions.

How would he react when she told him what she knew? Certainly on the face of it, knowing Erica's character, it was possible she'd been having an affair with Lucas. Sawyer knew about his wife's infidelities, but how could he know that one of his best friends might have been the one to betray him?

"How about some coffee?" he asked the minute

they walked into the silent house. "I'm not ready to call it a night yet."

"I have something else to tell you, something the bartender told me," she said with a touch of reluctance.

His dark green eyes held her gaze intently. "It must be something I'm not going to like, since you waited until now to tell me."

There was no way to find words to make it better, no way to soften what she had to say. "The bartender told me that a couple of times Lucas Jamison came in and Erica left with him."

She'd never thought it possible for his eyes to grow darker, but they did. Other than that his features gave nothing away of what he was feeling inside.

"Erica would have found it amusing to sleep with one of my friends," he finally said.

"But why would Lucas kill her? Is he married?" she asked.

He shook his head. "Divorced."

"Then he couldn't have been worried about her telling his wife." She frowned thoughtfully. "Maybe he was afraid people would find out that he was having an affair. Maybe he was afraid that would undermine his authority as sheriff."

"Lucas has a younger sister, Jenny, who is wild as a gator in heat. I can't imagine him worrying about what other people might think. I've changed my mind about the coffee. Go to bed, Amanda. I appreciate what you did tonight, but it's late and I'm sure you're tired."

She wasn't tired, but she had a feeling he wanted to be alone, to process what he'd just heard. "Then I'll just say good-night."

She left him there, standing in the foyer alone, as she suspected he'd been for a very long time. Once she was in her room, she paced the floor. She was too restless to go to bed and was surprised to realize she missed Melanie.

Each night before Melanie fell asleep, Amanda sat on the edge of her bed and talked. Although Melanie never uttered a word, there was communication happening between the two of them. Melanie communicated with her smiles, with a touch.

Most nights Amanda remained on the edge of the bed for long minutes after Melanie had fallen asleep. The motherless child who had seen something so traumatic that it had stolen her speech had somehow crawled into Amanda's heart.

She tried not to think of the other child, the one she'd lost, the one who had nearly destroyed her. With a deep sigh she moved to the window and stared outside into the dark of the night.

Sawyer was there, at the end of the dock, silhouetted against the dark swamp by the light from the back of the house. His shoulders were slumped and he looked like a man who had awakened in the middle of the night to find his life had vanished and he was alone.

She knew what that felt like. She knew the pain of realizing that nothing was as it should be, that everything you'd thought you had was stripped away by circumstances out of your control.

Without giving herself time to think, without wondering whether she was doing the right or the wrong thing, she left the room and headed for the stairs.

Once she was downstairs, she walked out the French doors that led outside and followed the path to the dock. He must have heard her approach. "I thought you were going to bed," he said without turning around.

"I thought maybe you needed to talk," she replied.

He did face her then, his features stark in the pale light. "I've just been wondering what I should have done differently. If I'd divorced Erica a year ago maybe none of this would have happened. Maybe she'd be off living the high life in Baton Rouge or New Orleans instead of dead."

"You can't blame yourself for what's happened. It was beyond your control. Sometimes life does that, it throws things at you that you just have to get through."

He tilted his head, his gaze not wavering from hers. "Is that why you're here? Did life throw things at you?"

She hesitated a moment, then nodded. "But that's a story for another time." A story she might never share with him.

He turned around once again. "I can't remember being afraid of much of anything in my life but right now the future scares the hell out of me."

There was nothing she could say, no platitudes

that wouldn't just be empty words. Instead of speaking, she stepped closer to him, wanting to bring comfort but unsure how to do it. Tentatively she moved to stand beside him and placed her hand on his arm.

He looked at her and his eyes gleamed almost silver. "You're a giver, aren't you, Amanda? I'll bet you're easy to take advantage of."

She looked at him in surprise. "I like to think of myself as being smart enough not to allow people to take advantage of me," she replied.

Turning to face her once again, he stepped so close to her she could smell the scent of beer on his breath and feel the heat of his body.

"You make a man want to take advantage of you." He reached out and touched a strand of her hair, then curled his fingers into it. The sultry night air seemed to press so tightly around them she couldn't draw a breath.

He released her hair and instead took her mouth with his. His lips were hard and demanding against hers, and she gave back to him with a hunger she hadn't known she'd possessed until he'd touched her.

The kiss ended as abruptly as it had begun. He ripped his mouth from hers and stepped back, his eyes holding the dark wildness of a predator. "Go inside, Amanda." Rough and commanding, his voice sliced through her. "Go inside before we both do something we're sure to regret."

She didn't think of doing anything other than

what he asked. With her heart racing and her lips still burning with the imprint of his, she turned and ran toward the house.

Chapter Six

Amanda was still in her room the next morning when she heard the familiar sound of footsteps running up the stairs. A moment later, Melanie burst through the door.

"Ah, you're home! I missed you," Amanda exclaimed.

Melanie grinned and walked over to the dry-erase board Amanda had hung on the wall. *I missed you, too,* she wrote with the marker.

"Did you have fun last night?" Amanda asked.

Melanie nodded, then walked over to Amanda and leaned into her. Amanda had worried that it was going to take time to break through Melanie's defenses, but she'd never met a child more ready to accept love. She seemed starved for it, and as Amanda gathered her into her arms, she realized there was a part of her that had been starved, as well.

"What are we going to do today?" she said. "Should we have a picnic? We could take lunch down to the dock and eat there." She wanted Melanie to recognize that the dock wasn't just a place of tragedy, but could be a place of fun once again.

Melanie tensed slightly, then slowly nodded her assent. "Good," Amanda said. "We'll see if Helen might make us something special for our picnic. And now it's probably time for breakfast." Even though it was Sunday, Helen would be in the kitchen. Sawyer had told Amanda that since Erica's death Helen had refused to take a day off, insisting that her place was here taking care of Melanie and Sawyer.

As she and Melanie made their way down the stairs to the dining room, Amanda steeled herself for seeing Sawyer. She had tossed and turned all night with the memory of that kiss and the knowledge that she hadn't wanted it to stop.

Thank God he'd had sense enough to halt things. For the moment his mouth had captured hers, all her sense had fled from her head.

When she and Amanda entered the dining room, Sawyer was already in his seat at the table sipping a cup of coffee. "Good morning," he said to Amanda, and she was grateful to see nothing of the darkness that had been in his eyes the night before.

"Good morning," she replied, and slid into her chair. "Melanie, I do believe I smell some of Helen's scrumptious cinnamon rolls."

"Indeed you do," Sawyer replied with a smile for his daughter. "Helen knows how much you like her cinnamon rolls."

Melanie nodded and rubbed her stomach.

"And we're going to have a picnic this afternoon down by the dock," Amanda said.

Sawyer's smile faltered a bit as he gazed at Melanie. "And that's okay with you?" As she had before, she hesitated a moment, then nodded her assent.

"The dock is such a pretty place," Amanda said, giving Sawyer a meaningful glance. "We can eat our lunch and smell the flowers and watch the fish flop and flash in the water."

"That sounds so nice I might just have to join you," Sawyer said.

Breakfast was pleasant with Sawyer and Amanda keeping up a running conversation about what they might see during their picnic. "I think we might see a raccoon eating a banana," Sawyer said, grinning at Melanie's resulting giggle.

"Or maybe a muskrat playing the fiddle," Amanda added.

The lightness of the conversation was welcome. Amanda had feared that things might be awkward this morning between Sawyer and herself, but there was nothing like laughter to banish awkwardness.

The humorous side of Sawyer was one she hadn't seen much of, but as he teased his daughter, Amanda found herself charmed by that side of him.

They had just finished breakfast but hadn't yet left the table when Helen ushered Lucas and a young deputy into the dining room. Instantly Amanda felt the tension rolling off Sawyer in waves.

"Helen, why don't you take Melanie into the kitchen with you," Sawyer said. A muscle ticked in his jaw as he gazed at the sheriff.

"Come on, darling. You can help me plan for that picnic lunch." Helen left the room with Melanie in tow.

"Lucas, what brings you out here so early on a Sunday morning?" Sawyer asked.

"I got a call this morning," Lucas replied. "An anonymous call."

The thick tension in the room made Amanda want to jump up and escape, but she remained frozen in her seat like a spectator watching a train wreck.

"And what did this caller have to say to you?" Sawyer asked.

Lucas shifted from one foot to the other. "The caller said that on the night that Erica was murdered you were seen burying something on the side of your shed. I brought along Deputy Maylor. We need to check it out, Sawyer."

"That's crap and you know it." Sawyer stood. "But fine, let's go check it out." He looked at Amanda. "I'd like you to come, too. It wouldn't hurt to have a witness."

"Tell me something, Lucas," Sawyer said as they walked toward the French doors. "Why would your caller wait this long to call in that kind of a tip?"

"I don't know. The caller didn't stay on the phone long enough for me to ask any questions,"

Lucas replied. "It sounded like the voice was disguised, could have been a man or a woman. I know it's probably nothing more than a crank call, but as an officer of the law you know it's my duty to check it out."

They stepped out into the steamy sunshine and headed toward the shed. It wasn't until they reached the outbuilding that Sawyer broke the uncomfortable silence that had sprung up between them all.

"Tell me something else, Lucas," he said, his voice deceptively soft. "Was it your duty as an officer of the law to sleep with my wife?"

Lucas's handsome features blanched, and he halted in his tracks and faced Sawyer. "What in the hell are you talking about? I never slept with Erica. You should know me better than that." A rich anger rocked through his voice.

"I'm talking about the fact that I've heard that twice before her death Erica was seen leaving Cajun Country in your company." Sawyer didn't raise his voice, but his own anger was visible in the tight clench of his hands at his sides, in the rigid posture as he faced his friend.

The young deputy looked down at the ground, as if wishing he were anywhere but here.

"That's true," Lucas said, the anger appearing to seep out of him as he drew a weary sigh. "Jenny was going through a bad time. She'd broken up with some loser of a boyfriend and was talking suicide. You know she was crazy about Erica, so I asked

Erica to talk to her. That's all it was, Sawyer. I swear to God it wasn't about me, it was about Jenny."

Sawyer said nothing, and Amanda wondered what he was thinking, if he believed Lucas.

"The Brotherhood, Sawyer," Lucas said softly. "Just because college is long behind us do you think I could forget the bonds we forged? The promises we made to each other? I'd never sleep with your wife. That's not the kind of man I am."

"And I didn't kill her," Sawyer said. "Because that's not the kind of man I am."

Some of the tension eased, and Amanda drew her first full breath since the conversation had begun.

Sawyer pointed toward the shed. "Go on, check whatever you need to check."

Amanda's heartbeat raced as they moved to the east side of the shed, and the deputy and Lucas began to survey the ground. For the first time Amanda realized that Deputy Maylor held a small spade in his hand, ready to dig up whatever might have been buried.

Lucas walked back and forth along the side of the shed, his gaze intently focused on the ground. "Here," Lucas said, and pointed to an area of ground that looked different than the rest. The grass wasn't as green, and the patch was slightly higher than the areas around it. Maylor bent down and began to dig in the soil.

For several long moments the only sound was that of the spade against the earth. The deputy moved the dirt tentatively as if not wanting to disturb the treasure he might find.

Amanda wanted to scream at him to hurry up, to get this over with. She prayed there was nothing there, but the silent plea had barely left her head when the spade hit something foreign.

Clink.

Amanda's heart seemed to stop beating. Deputy Maylor glanced up at Sawyer, then worked the spade to uncover what had been buried. A knife. Sawyer hissed in surprise and stumbled back a step.

"Maylor, go get an evidence bag," Lucas said.

"Somebody is setting me up," Sawyer said as the young deputy strode off in the direction of the patrol car. "I didn't bury that knife." The timber of his voice indicated not only how stunned he was by the discovery of the knife, but also how upset he was. "I've never even seen that thing before."

Amanda stared at the knife. The blade was about six inches long and had on it what appeared to be rust, but what she knew was dried blood. The handle was what looked like mother-of-pearl, although it was difficult to be sure with the dirt clinging to it.

There was no doubt in her mind that this was the missing murder weapon. Somebody had used that knife to stab Erica, then had buried it here where it would point yet another finger at Sawyer.

"Am I going to be arrested?" Sawyer faced Lucas, his features taut with strain.

Emotion pressed against Amanda's chest, and

unexpected tears burned at her eyes. The silly picnic chatter seemed like a lifetime ago as she waited for Lucas to answer Sawyer's question.

Lucas released a deep sigh and stared off toward the swamp. "I find it damned suspicious that I got that call this morning. I also wonder how anyone could have seen you do anything on the night of the murder. This isn't exactly a highly populated area."

He looked at Sawyer once again. "I'll send the knife to the lab, see what they can get off it. At this point we don't know if it is the murder weapon and we can't even determine if the knife was buried the night of Erica's murder or a month before, or last week for that matter. For the time being you aren't under arrest. We'll see what the lab results are. In the meantime I don't have to tell you that you need to stick around, don't leave town."

He hesitated a moment, then continued, "If you haven't contacted a lawyer, get one now. I'm not the only one driving this train, Sawyer. I told you before that the district attorney and the mayor are both pushing for your arrest. Get your things in order, because I don't know how much longer I can keep you out of jail."

"Are we done here?" Sawyer asked. When Lucas nodded, Sawyer turned on his heels and headed for the house. Amanda hurried after him.

He went directly to the kitchen. "Where's Melanie?" he asked Helen.

"She went up to her room," Helen replied.

As Sawyer took the stairs, Amanda was at his heels. The energy that rolled off him felt dark and sick and she worried about his intent.

Melanie turned as they entered her room, her little smile fading as Sawyer strode over to her and knelt down before her. "Melanie, you have to talk now," he said, a crazed urgency in his voice. "You have to tell Daddy what you saw the night that Mommy died." He grabbed her by the shoulders and her eyes widened in alarm. "Tell me, Melanie. You must tell me now."

"Sawyer!" Amanda shoved between him and his daughter. "Stop it!" she exclaimed.

He stood, his eyes wild. "Get out of my way. I'm talking to my daughter."

"No, you're frightening your daughter and I won't allow it."

His eyes blazed and his nostrils flared. "You won't allow it? I think you forget your place here."

"Then maybe I don't have a place here," Amanda replied, equally as angry.

"Fine, pack your bags." He didn't wait for her reply but whirled around and stalked out of the bedroom.

For a long moment Amanda remained frozen in place, wondering how things had so quickly flamed out of control. Was she fired? He'd hired her to take care of Melanie. She couldn't just stand by and watch while he browbeat her. Her job was to protect Melanie's mental health, and that included protecting her from a father who had obviously just had a momentary meltdown.

She turned to face Melanie, her pale little face radiating stress. Amanda sat on the edge of the bed and motioned the child into her arms. Melanie came into her embrace eagerly and buried her head against Amanda's heart.

"Your daddy didn't mean to yell at you," Amanda said as she smoothed her hand over the softness of Melanie's dark hair. "He was just upset, that's all. He was upset and he misses the sound of your voice."

Pack your bags.

The words reverberated through her head. Had he meant it? Was she now supposed to gather her things and leave? Just like that?

She tightened her arms around Melanie. Melanie raised her head and looked at Amanda with tear-filled eyes.

"Don't go."

For an instant Amanda wasn't sure if she'd actually heard the whispered words or merely imagined them. She stared at Melanie and watched as her lips formed the words again. "Please, don't go."

Amanda once again tightened her arms around Melanie. "Don't worry, sweetheart, I'm not going anywhere," she said firmly.

Now all she had to do was tell Sawyer that she was staying and then she'd let him know that his daughter had finally spoken.

SAWYER STOOD at the window in his office, staring out at the shed in the distance, guilt ripping him in half. God, he'd lost it. Worse, he'd lost it with his daughter.

His head filled with a vision of Melanie, her eyes wide with fear and her body trembling as he'd demanded she speak. She'd been afraid of him. Of him!

What had he been thinking? How could he have done that to her? She'd been through enough without having a father yell and scream at her.

He moved away from the window and sat in the chair behind his desk. He dropped his head into his hands. He knew if the sheriff was anyone other than Lucas, he would already be behind bars. Still there was no way that knife would yield his fingerprints. He'd never seen it before the deputy had dug it up. He prayed there were other fingerprints on it. The killer's fingerprints.

Who had made that anonymous call? Who was trying to frame him for his wife's murder? The real murderer, of course, but who? Dammit, who could it be?

Melanie. He needed to go back up and apologize to her…and to Amanda. She'd shocked him, jumping between him and Melanie like a mother bear protecting her cub.

Now that the heat of the moment had passed and he'd regained the senses that had momentarily fled, he realized he admired Amanda for that. He liked the fact that she'd jumped in to protect Melanie despite the consequences she might face from him.

And he'd told her to pack her bags. He got up from the desk. He needed to tell her he was sorry. Before he could get around the desk, she appeared in his doorway.

"Amanda."

Her chin was raised in a gesture of battle. "I'm not leaving." Her eyes glittered with emotion. "Melanie doesn't want me to go. She needs me. And you might not know it but you need me to be here for her."

"You're right." His words appeared to take some of the defensive wind out of her. "And I owe you an apology. I don't know what got into me. I can't believe I acted like that to you, but more importantly, to Melanie."

"Apology accepted," she replied.

He looked at her in surprise. "That easily?"

"I'm not one to hold a grudge. Besides, I know that wasn't you upstairs. That was a man pushed to the edge by the discovery of a murder weapon in his backyard."

Sawyer rubbed the center of his forehead, where a headache throbbed with dull intensity. "I don't know how to fight this. I don't know what to do next to help myself."

She stepped closer to him, her features radiating a deep empathy. "Did you believe Lucas? About Erica?"

Sawyer dropped his hand from his forehead. "I'd like to believe him, but truthfully I don't know what to believe. There are really only two people I'm sure had nothing to do with Erica's death, and that's you and Melanie. Beyond that I can't afford to trust anyone."

"Whoever made that anonymous call to Lucas killed Erica," she said. "Surely Lucas realizes that."

"If there was an anonymous call." For all he knew Lucas had buried that knife a week before, then had pretended to get a call. He sighed, his suspicions exhausting him. "Where's Melanie? I need to apologize to her."

"She's back in the kitchen with Helen supervising the preparations for our picnic. And before you talk to her I need to tell you something about her."

"Okay. What?"

She paused a moment, and fear bubbled up inside him. "Is she okay?" Dear God, was she going to tell him that Melanie didn't want to see him? That he'd further traumatized his daughter with his actions?

"She's fine," Amanda assured him. "But after you left the bedroom, she spoke."

Sawyer stared at her, wanting to believe, needing to believe that finally the wall around Melanie had tumbled down. "Wh-what did she say?" The emotion that rose up inside him had nothing to do with the fact that his daughter might be able to tell the authorities what she'd seen. Rather it was the pure joy in knowing that his daughter had taken a step toward healing.

"She said, 'Don't go.'"

"Did she say anything else?"

Amanda shook her head. "I tried to get her to say more, but that was all. It wasn't much, but it was a breakthrough. Still, the worst thing we can do right now is to push her in any way."

"Believe me, there will not be a repeat of my earlier performance with my daughter."

Amanda's blue eyes soothed him. He'd never met a woman who had such a core of calm inside her. "So, what happens now?" she asked.

"We live our lives. We enjoy each moment we have because we both know that at any time Lucas could show up at the front door with handcuffs for me. In the meantime I'll try to figure out who is the guilty party."

Once again he was nearly overwhelmed with a sense of helplessness as he realized that his freedom was tenuous at best.

And unless he thought of some way to find Erica's killer, he might not be around to hear his daughter say another word.

Chapter Seven

It was a gorgeous Friday afternoon, and Amanda sat at the patio table sipping a glass of iced tea. Sawyer had taken the afternoon off from work and had come home to take his daughter to a movie. He'd asked Amanda to come along, but she'd declined, believing that father and daughter could use some quality time alone. Melanie hadn't spoken since that one time.

It had been five long days since the knife had been dug up by the shed. Each minute of each day she had feared the knock on the door that would take Sawyer away, but so far that knock hadn't come.

Sawyer had contacted his college friend Jackson Burdeaux to represent him if and when he was charged with the murder.

She stared off toward the dock and remembered the kiss they had shared. There had been several times during the past week that she'd thought he was about to kiss her again, but each time, he'd moved away from her and the moment had passed.

Taking another sip of her tea, she acknowledged to herself that she'd wanted him to kiss her again, that Sawyer Bennett was crawling as deeply into her heart as his daughter had.

It was foolishness to allow herself to feel anything for him other than that of employee for employer. Certainly his future didn't look bright and to get involved with him on a romantic level could lead only to utter heartbreak.

The French doors opened and Helen stepped out, carrying a small platter of freshly baked sugar cookies. "Thought you might like a little something sweet to go with that tea."

"Thank you, Helen," Amanda replied, pleased that the dour woman appeared to be warming up to her. "Why don't you sit for a minute and eat one with me." Amanda gestured to the chair opposite her at the table.

Helen hesitated a moment, then sat and reached for one of the cookies. "These are Melanie's favorites," she said. "That little girl has a sweet tooth like her daddy."

"You've worked for Sawyer for a long time?"

"I worked for his parents for ten years before I came here to work for him." She frowned, her gray eyebrows knitting together across her brow. "I know they're spinning in their graves right now, knowing that their son is in trouble."

She bit into the cookie, then continued. "They knew that woman was trouble the minute he brought her home to meet them. Thank the Lord they died before he married her and all this evil happened."

"How did they die?" Amanda asked, curious to know anything and everything about Sawyer.

"A plane crash. Mr. Bennett, he loved to fly, and he'd chartered a small plane to take him and Mrs. Bennett from here to Shreveport. Something went wrong and the plane went down. Killed both the Bennetts and the pilot. Damn shame it was. Sawyer took it real hard and married that woman soon after."

When Sawyer had talked about his marriage to Erica, he hadn't mentioned that before their wedding he'd recently lost his parents. How much had that loss played into his decision to marry Erica?

Helen stood. "I've got to get back to the kitchen." She started to walk off, then turned back to Amanda. "Melanie, she's all I worry about. That baby girl has already had too much bad in her life. I misjudged you. I thought you'd be gone by now. I think you're stronger than I realized." With that she turned on her heels and disappeared back into the house.

Amanda grabbed one of the cookies from the platter and munched thoughtfully. Helen certainly didn't hide the fact that she'd hated Erica. Was it possible that Helen had removed Erica from Melanie's life? Was it possible that it had been Helen who had met Erica on the dock that night and stabbed her to death?

She frowned, realizing she was grasping at straws. It was difficult to seriously imagine a wom-

an who baked sugar cookies being capable of stab-
bing a woman to death. Besides, Helen was an
elderly woman, surely she wouldn't have had the
strength to attack Erica.

But Amanda had seen her hack up a chicken with
a minimum of effort. She'd seen Helen's strong
forearms as she rolled out pie dough. She sighed,
recognizing that every person she met was a potential suspect. What must it be like for Sawyer, who
had to suspect every friend he held dear.

Amanda raised her face to the sun. As always, the
thought of Erica's murder sent a bone-shivering
chill through her. The murder had been brutal. Erica
had been stabbed multiple times, indicating a hatred, a rage that had been out of control.

She was just about to go back inside when Lillian
appeared at the edge of the woods that separated the
Bennett house from the Cordells. She waved as she
approached where Amanda had sunk back in her
chair in surprise.

"You look like a wood nymph," Amanda exclaimed as Lillian reached her.

Lillian laughed. "There's a path through the
woods between the houses. I felt like a walk and
thought I'd come over for a visit."

Amanda smiled and gestured toward the chair
Helen had recently vacated. "I've just been sitting
enjoying the peace and quiet."

"Where's Melanie?"

"Sawyer took her to a movie."

"And you didn't go?" Lillian reached out and took one of the last cookies from the platter and bit into it with an audible sigh of pleasure.

"I thought it would be nice for them to spend some time alone together," Amanda replied.

"Tough week?"

Amanda released a dry laugh. "That would be an understatement." She sighed, her smile dropping from her lips. "It's just difficult knowing that at any moment a knock on the door could mean Sawyer's arrest."

Lillian took a moment to chew the cookie, then brushed the crumbs from her lap. "I heard they found the murder weapon here on the property."

Amanda sat up straighter in the chair. "Where did you hear that? I didn't know that information had been released to the public."

It was Lillian's turn to laugh drily. "Honey, Conja Creek might be a town of affluent, privileged people but underneath the civilized surface beats the heart of a small town, and there's nothing a small town loves more than juicy gossip." She reached for another of the cookies and continued, "I heard it from Suzette when she was doing my hair. I think her son works as a dispatcher or something at the sheriff's office."

"They dug up a knife next to the shed. They're waiting for lab results to determine if it was the murder weapon, but Sawyer and I are certain it is."

"How's he dealing with things?"

Amanda stared off into the distance, then looked

back at Lillian. "He's dealing with everything as best he can. Jackson Burdeaux came by on Wednesday and he and Sawyer holed up for most of the day."

"Now there's a piece of work," Lillian exclaimed.

"Who? Jackson? He seemed very nice." Amanda thought of the criminal defense attorney. Dark hair and handsome as the devil, he'd had warm gray eyes that had instantly put Amanda at ease.

"Don't let his good-ol'-boy Southern charm fool you. The man is a cunning shark in the courtroom."

"Good," Amanda said fervently. "That's exactly what Sawyer needs, a shark who can keep an innocent man out of prison."

"Anything else new?" Lillian asked.

Amanda thought about telling her that Melanie had finally spoken, but then decided not to. After all, it had only been a couple of words and she hadn't said anything since then. "No, not really."

"And you two didn't learn anything the night you went to Cajun Country?"

"No, the bartender told me that Erica had stopped coming in there several months before her death." Amanda leaned forward, gazing at Lillian intently. "You and Erica were so close. Are you sure she never told you who she was sleeping with?"

"Erica told me a lot of her secrets. I knew when she spent money she wasn't supposed to spend, when she shamelessly flirted with a man she shouldn't. I knew she sometimes drank too much and loved to have sex in places where the chance of getting caught was high. She once had a lover in my studio when I was at the store. She bragged about it later but refused to tell me who the man was. She'd never tell me names of her lovers. That was a secret she absolutely refused to share."

"It's a secret I'd love to know. Sawyer and I both think that whoever she was sleeping with at the time of her death is her killer. It was obviously a crime of passion. She wasn't just killed, it was overkill." Amanda fought against a new chill.

Lillian visibly shivered, as if the cold that had gripped Amanda's heart had somehow transferred to her. "You know what really freaks me out?"

"What's that?"

"That somebody I probably know is a murderer. That somebody, a friend or a neighbor, had the capacity to do that to Erica." Tears filled Lillian's eyes. "She didn't deserve what happened to her. She had faults, yes, but she shouldn't have died."

Amanda reached across the table and covered one of Lillian's hands with hers. "I'm sorry. I shouldn't have been talking about this."

Lillian shook her head and squeezed her eyes tightly closed, then gulped air and looked at Amanda. "No, it's all right. We have to figure out who did this. I'm just afraid…" She pulled her hand from Amanda's and let her voice trail off.

"Afraid of what?"

Lillian looked out toward the swamp, toward the place where her best friend had been murdered.

When she looked back at Amanda, her gaze was troubled. "I hate to even say it out loud," she said, her voice a faint whisper.

"Say what?"

She hesitated and when she finally spoke again her voice was still a mere whisper. "I'm beginning to think that Sawyer did it. I'm beginning to think that Sawyer killed Erica."

THE NIGHT-LIGHT CAST a silvery glow in Melanie's bedroom. Amanda sat on the edge of the bed, watching the little girl as she slept.

It had been a busy Sunday. Sawyer had invited half a dozen of his friends and supporters to dinner. James and Lillian had been there, as had Jackson Burdeaux and Sawyer's business partner, Adam Kincaid, and his wife, Stella.

Although the food had been excellent and the conversation benign and pleasant, Amanda had been unable to shake the feeling that somehow this was their Last Supper. She thought that Sawyer had decided to call together the important people in his life because he knew his freedom was quickly coming to an end.

She now drew a deep breath, taking in the little-girl scent of Melanie. With each day that passed, she knew it would be more and more difficult to tell Melanie goodbye. And more and more difficult to say goodbye to Sawyer.

She'd spent the past twenty-four hours thinking

about Lillian's startling whispered confession. Although she'd tried to get Lillian to tell her why she doubted Sawyer's innocence, Lillian had stubbornly changed the subject.

Funny, Lillian's doubts had done nothing to shake Amanda's belief in Sawyer's innocence. Her belief in him and his innocence only grew stronger the more she got to know him. Each night when the two of them talked he shared pieces of himself that let her know what kind of man he was, and he was a good man, an honorable man.

Knowing that Melanie was sound asleep, she stood and stretched with her arms overhead, the book she'd been reading to Melanie still clutched in one hand. She was tired, but still needed to go downstairs and check in with Sawyer.

She moved to the bookshelf and reached up to the top shelf, where a pink-and-white photo box worked as a bookend to hold up a small collection of books. As she nudged the book in with the others, she bumped the box, which toppled to the floor.

She shot a glance to Melanie but apparently the sound hadn't awakened her. Thank goodness, she thought as she knelt to pick up the contents that had spilled out.

Obviously, the box hadn't contained photos. The first item she grabbed was a gold cigarette lighter. In the pale illumination from the night-light she stared at the items in confusion. It was kind of like peering into somebody's junk drawer. Besides the lighter there was a silver chain that appeared to be a man's bracelet. Matchbooks and a brass candle-holder nestled next to an empty gold picture frame and a monogrammed towel.

Amanda's heart pounded. This wasn't something that belonged to an eight-year-old girl. These items weren't things that Melanie had saved in the box then placed on the highest shelf in the room.

This container belonged to Erica and had been hidden in plain sight, in a pretty pink-and-white box that matched the decor in her daughter's room.

Souvenirs? Was it possible these items were souvenirs from Erica's affairs? That was the only thing that made sense.

With a galloping heartbeat, she placed the lid back on, then picked up the container and carried it out of the room.

Maybe by looking through the items they could figure out who Erica had been sleeping with. Maybe inside the container was the clue that would finally lead them to a murderer. Her heart raced just a little faster.

She hurried down the stairs to find Sawyer. Most evenings at this time he was in his office, but tonight he wasn't there.

She found him in the kitchen, drinking a cup of coffee and staring out the back window as if in a daze. "Sawyer?"

He turned to look at her. "What have you got there?"

Setting the container down on the table, she smiled. For the first time since she'd arrived hope filled her up. "I think maybe I found what we were looking for when we searched Erica's room. I think she kept keepsakes of her affairs, and they're in here." She thumped the top of the box with her fingers.

He stood and moved to stand next to her, his gaze riveted on the container. "Where did you find it?"

"On the top bookshelf in Melanie's room. I was putting the book away that I'd read to her earlier and accidentally knocked it off the shelf." She smiled apologetically. "My natural nosiness got the best of me so I looked through the contents."

"Thank God for that nosiness. Let's see what's inside." Tension made his voice deeper than usual.

Amanda pulled open the lid and watched as Sawyer got his first look at the contents. His features displayed no emotion as he picked up first one item, then another.

"Anything look familiar?" she asked.

He frowned and picked up the gold cigarette lighter. A large silver star decorated one side. "This looks kind of familiar, but I'm not sure where I've seen it before. At least a half a dozen of my friends and acquaintances are smokers."

He set the lighter down and grabbed a small picture frame decorated with hearts and flowers. "I'm sure I've seen this somewhere before but I don't know where." He grabbed one of the matchbooks. "The Night Owl Motel. Not exactly a five-star establishment."

"But maybe we could go there and ask some questions, see if the clerk remembers Erica and whoever she might have been with."

"I guess it's worth a try." He rummaged around and picked up a total of four matchbooks from four different motels. "Maybe somebody at one of these places will remember something." He grabbed the monogrammed hand towel with the initials WWW.

"You know anyone that might belong to?" she asked.

He traced the raised black lettering with the tip of his index finger. "WWW. World Wide Web?" he said half-jokingly.

"Somehow I don't think that's what it stands for," she replied.

He shook his head. "Offhand I can't think of anybody I know with those initials."

Amanda grabbed Sawyer's arm, excitement flooding through her. "This is it, Sawyer. Surely this is what we've been searching for, what we've needed. We have something now, something we can investigate, something that I'm sure will lead us to the guilty party."

His eyes glowed with the first hope she'd seen all week. "Maybe you're right. Maybe the answer to who killed Erica is inside this pretty box." He covered her hand with his, and the warmth of his touch shot straight through to her heart.

"I brought you here for Melanie, but I'm not sure what I would have done without you for the past two weeks," he said. With his free hand he reached up and touched her cheek. "Somehow you've managed to keep me sane through the worst days of my life."

She turned her face into the palm of his hand. She'd been hungry for his touch since the night they'd shared that single, searing kiss.

It took only one look at his face to see his hunger, and she knew he intended to kiss her again. And she wanted his kiss. Even knowing there was no real permanent place for her here. Even knowing she was probably just a convenience for him, a temporary fix against loneliness.

When his mouth crashed down on hers, she accepted the kiss with a hunger of her own. As his arms wrapped around her waist and pulled her close against him, she twined her fingers into his hair, loving the way the silky strands felt against her fingertips.

He held her close enough to mold their bodies together, close enough that she could feel he was aroused. Tomorrow Lucas Jamison might knock on the door and Sawyer would be taken away and possibly never return again.

But tonight he was here with her, and she told herself that a single night with him would be enough, that she could live with this night and the promise of nothing more.

He deepened his kiss, his tongue sliding into her mouth with delicious intent. She met the thrust of his tongue with her own, her heart crashing in a rhythm of half-forgotten desire.

She couldn't remember the last time she'd wanted a man as she did him. The intensity of her desire half frightened her. It wasn't the spell of Conja Creek that thickened her blood and raced her pulse, rather it was the spell of Sawyer.

He broke the kiss with a gasp and dropped his hands to his sides. His eyes gleamed with the wildness of a primal forest as he gazed at her. "I want you, Amanda. I want you in my bed, naked in my arms. But it wouldn't be fair."

"To who? Who wouldn't it be fair to, Sawyer? To you? If you want me, then it can't be wrong to have me. To me? I understand the risks. I know that we can make love tonight, and tomorrow I may have to pack my bags and leave. But it's a risk I'm willing to take."

His gaze searched her face as if looking for doubt, for hesitation. She knew he would find none. He held out his hand to her and she grasped it, and together, without saying another word, they walked toward the stairs.

How many mistakes could you make in one lifetime? she wondered as they climbed the stairs, then walked the long hallway to the master bedroom.

Certainly her relationship with Scott had been a major mistake. She'd thought him to be a strong, honorable man who loved her but he'd shown himself to be a weak coward who had run when her world had begun to crumble.

Sawyer tightened his grip on her hand as they reached the door to his bedroom. She'd misjudged the man Scott had been, and somewhere in the back of her mind she realized that, if she'd misjudged Sawyer, as well, then it was possible she was about to make love to a man who had committed murder.

Chapter Eight

Where Erica's room had been an explosion of color and energy, Sawyer's bedroom held a subtle masculinity. A black-and-gray spread covered the king-size bed, and massive dark wood nightstands stood sentry on either side.

A single lamp burned on one of the nightstands, casting shadows on the walls of the room as they stepped inside. Sawyer dropped her hand and faced her, his features radiating his want but also a calm acceptance of whatever might happen.

"It's not too late for you to go to your own room," he said, his voice gentle. "I'll understand. You found that box of Erica's things. Our emotions flew out of control."

The fact that he was giving her an opportunity to change her mind, to save face and make a hasty exit, only made her want him more. She stepped closer to him and placed her hand on his jaw, enjoying the faint brush of whiskers beneath her palm.

"I don't want to go back to my room," she replied, her voice thick with her own emotion. "I want to be with you, Sawyer."

The words barely left her before his mouth crashed down on hers once again and the hunger that had simmered inside her for him exploded out of control.

He pulled her against him, his mouth ravishing hers as his hands caressed her back and cupped her buttocks. When he drew her hips into his, she gasped with the knowledge that he was fully aroused.

The kiss seemed to last a lifetime, and yet when he pulled his mouth from hers she felt bereft, as if the kiss hadn't lasted nearly long enough.

She grabbed the bottom of his T-shirt, wanting it off him, needing to feel the strength and warmth of his bare chest against hers. He accommodated her, ripping the shirt up and over his head.

As he walked to the side of the bed and pulled down the spread, she unbuttoned her blouse and shrugged it off her shoulders. It fell to the floor as he turned back to look at her, and his eyes glowed with a heat she felt from her head to her toes.

"You are beautiful," he said.

Amanda had never thought of herself as beautiful. She knew she was reasonably attractive, but nothing exceptional. But beneath his gaze she felt beautiful. He made her feel sexy and feminine, desired in a way she couldn't remember ever feeling before.

They removed the rest of their clothes and fell

onto the bed, legs and arms atangle as lips met in another fiery kiss. As his hands cupped her breasts, her nipples rose to meet his touch and she moaned with pleasure.

Every nerve in her body was electrified as his mouth left hers and rained soft, nipping kisses along her jawline and down the length of her neck.

As he explored her with his hands and lips, she did the same to him, running her fingers through the thatch of dark, curly hair on his chest, tasting the warmth and texture of his skin.

Wildness. It seemed to infuse them both. And it didn't take long before he took a condom from his nightstand, put it on, then moved between her thighs. She was ready for him. She felt as if she'd been ready for him from the first moment they had met.

He slid into her, then froze, every muscle in his body tensed. He gazed down at her, his features taut and his dark green eyes gleaming. He whispered her name with a tenderness that threatened to bring tears to her eyes.

She placed her hands on the sides of his face, and he bent his head down and kissed her. When the kiss ended he moved his hips, thrusting into her as a low groan issued from his throat.

All thoughts of murders and arrests and silent little girls vanished as she gave herself to the pleasure of their lovemaking.

It didn't take long for her to feel the slow build of tension coiling in the very depths of her. Sawyer seemed to sense it and quickened his strokes. She gasped and clung to him, her fingers biting into his back as waves of pleasure crashed through her.

She gasped out his name and shuddered with the force of her release. Seconds later he stiffened against her and moaned as he found his own release.

He rolled off her and onto his back, both of them gasping in an effort to regain a normal heartbeat. "I'll be right back," he said. "Don't go anywhere." He got out of bed and padded into the adjoining bathroom.

She smiled. She couldn't have moved if a bomb exploded in the middle of the room. Her limbs felt like noodles, weak from the exertion.

He returned a moment later and slid back beneath the sheets and gathered her against him in an embrace. She snuggled against his side, loving the warmth of him, the scent of him.

"I told myself it would be selfish of me to make love to you," he said.

"It would have been selfish of you not to since I wanted it as badly as you," she replied.

He tightened his arm around her and released a deep sigh and she knew with that sigh that the outside world had come back to them.

"Amanda, I don't know where we go from here."

"We go back to what we've been doing. I take care of Melanie, you do what you need to do to get through each day, and we try to find out who killed Erica."

He laughed. "You make it sound easy."

She raised her head to look at him. "If you're

worried about what I might expect or demand because of what happened tonight, then stop worrying. I understand the situation, Sawyer. I don't expect anything to be different just because we fell into bed together. What we need to focus on is finding out who owned those items in that box."

"I guess I need to call Lucas and turn it all over to him. But before I do I want an inventory of everything that's in that box."

"I can make a detailed inventory first thing in the morning," she replied.

"After you do that I'll turn those things over. Maybe Lucas can figure out something that we can't."

"We need to check out those motels, see if maybe a clerk will remember seeing Erica checking in with a man."

He smiled again. "Were you a private detective in another lifetime?"

"Maybe, but if I was I have no memories of it. All I know is that we have to find the proof that you're innocent, and the only way to do that is to find the real killer."

"Finding a killer definitely wasn't in your job description," he replied.

"I know, but taking care of Melanie was, and I don't want to see her lose her father." There were so many other things she could have said, like the fact that she couldn't bear the thought of him behind bars, like the fact that *she* didn't want to lose him, either.

And with this thought she knew she had allowed

herself to get too close, not only physically but mentally, as well.

She sidled away from him. "I need to get back to my own bed," she said. "I don't want Melanie to wake up in the morning and not find me where I belong."

He didn't stop her as she slid out of the bed, grabbed her clothes from the floor, then disappeared into his bathroom.

She stared at her reflection in the mirror above the sink. Cheeks flushed, eyes shining, she looked like a woman who had just been thoroughly, wonderfully loved.

You're nothing but a rebound for him, a little voice whispered in her head. *He's going through the worst possible time of his life and you're an easy convenience to release stress, to feel not quite so all alone.*

Even knowing all this she couldn't regret what they had just shared. She turned away from the mirror and pulled on her clothes, then stepped back out of the bathroom and into the bedroom where Sawyer hadn't moved from the bed.

He sat up, the sheet slipping down to expose his firmly muscled chest. "Are you all right?"

"I'm fine." But she wasn't. She suddenly needed to escape the room, to escape him. "I'll see you in the morning." She turned and left the room, then hurried down the hallway to her own bedroom.

A glimpse into Melanie's room let her know the little girl was sound asleep. Amanda pulled off her clothes once again and got into her nightgown, but she knew sleep would be a long time coming.

Her mind whirled with all the events of the night. The discovery of the box of Erica's odd keepsakes, the euphoria of a real dose of hope and finally the exquisite pleasure of Sawyer all battled in her head.

You're just an easy convenience, that little voice whispered once again. And she'd do well to remember that, to not put any weight into what they had shared tonight. When all was said and done, she was still just an employee, a nanny hired to help his daughter through a rough time.

She sat on the edge of her bed and wondered what Sawyer would think if he knew about the tragic event that had forced her to leave Kansas City.

She'd certainly given him the benefit of the doubt where his guilt was concerned. Would he be as willing to do the same for her?

She drifted to the window and peered out onto the moonlit landscape. She froze as she saw somebody standing on the dock, somebody whose shape was far too broad to be Sawyer's.

George.

What was he doing there? As she watched he turned to face the house, and she could feel his gaze focused on her window. She stepped back, heart beating fast and furious.

She peered out once again, knowing that he couldn't see her, as her room was darker than the night outside. He still stood there, still as a statue, watching…as if waiting.

Waiting for what? She left the window and wrapped her arms around herself to warm the bone-chilling shiver that worked up her spine.

SAWYER SAT AT HIS DESK in his Baton Rouge office, staring out the tenth-floor window into the blue skies outside. In his hand he held the gold lighter that had been in the box Amanda had found the night before.

He'd taken the lighter out before leaving for work that morning. He'd awakened before dawn and had known who the lighter belonged to. It was as if during the night, while he'd slept, his subconscious had worked to give him the answer.

The flame leaped to life with a flick of his thumb. He should have called Lucas this morning, told him about the box, told him about the lighter. He moved his thumb, and the flame extinguished. He should have called Lucas but he hadn't. He rubbed his finger over the raised silver star that decorated the side of the lighter.

There was a cold hard knot in his chest, a knot of anger he hadn't felt since the night of Erica's death. He felt as if for the past couple of months, since that dreadful night, he had stopped participating in his own life, had gone into a place where all his senses, all his emotions were numbed.

But last night, holding Amanda in his arms,

feeling the warmth of her skin against his, her fevered sighs against his neck, he'd realized how much he wanted a life, his life back. And he wasn't sure that Lucas could get it back for him.

He'd be a fool to trust anyone at this point. Despite their brotherhood and friendship, even Lucas was a suspect at this point. Sawyer had no idea who might have been snared in Erica's web and to what lengths they might have gone to extract themselves.

Before last night there had been a part of him that hadn't wanted to know who Erica had slept with. He hadn't wanted to know the names, see the faces of the men with whom she'd betrayed her marriage vows.

Now he wanted to know them all, knew in his gut that among them was a monster. He flicked the lighter once again and the flame jumped up. He let it burn until the lighter got hot, then he allowed it to go out.

Amanda. She leaped into his mind as he tossed the lighter onto the top of his desk. They had both been foolish last night. They should never have taken their relationship from professional to intimate. His life was in chaos, and even if it wasn't, he wasn't sure he was prepared to jump into another relationship.

Last night hadn't been fair to her. The only thing that consoled him was the fact that she seemed to know the score. She'd made it clear that she expected nothing more from him than what he'd given her.

And it wouldn't happen again. One mistake was bad enough. Eventually this would all be over. Melanie would be talking again, she'd go back to school and they wouldn't need Amanda anymore. Funny, how the thought of Amanda not being in the house, not being a part of their lives in some form or another bothered him.

As he heard the outer office door whoosh open, all thoughts of Amanda flew from his mind. He grabbed the lighter from the desk and stuck it in his shirt pocket.

A rap of knuckles sounded on his door, then it opened and Adam swept in, a broad smile on his face. "We got it, partner!"

"Got what?"

Adam sat in the chair opposite Sawyer's desk. "We got the Ribideaux account." He jumped back up, as if too excited to sit. "It's huge. They want condominiums and shops, restaurants and lots of green space. They want to see tentative plans in a month."

"That's great," Sawyer replied. "Why don't we go down to the Drum Room and have a celebration drink?"

"Sounds good. We deserve a celebration."

They left the office together, Adam chattering on about the new project. He'd been courting Samuel Ribideaux for the past six months, knowing that the wealthy developer was in the process of putting together a plan for a huge project.

He continued to talk as they walked into the elevator that would take them to the bottom floor of the building. In the evenings and on weekends, the

Drum Room was a popular singles hangout, but during the day it was a place for businesspeople to meet over lunch or for drinks.

As they rode down, Sawyer imagined he could feel the heat of the lighter burning a hole in his pocket. A muscle ticked in his jaw as he eyed Adam. He and Adam had been business partners for seven years. Their firm of Bennett and Kincaid had been quite successful, particularly over the past two years.

The job for Ribideaux was an indication of the fact that they had truly arrived, that their reputation for excellence was firmly in place.

At the moment, Sawyer didn't give a damn about the business or the Ribideaux project. After all, if things didn't change, he wouldn't be around to enjoy whatever success the new project would bring.

The elevator doors opened, and he and Adam stepped out and headed to the hallway that led into a back entrance of the Drum Room.

The scent of cooking food and cigarette smoke hung in the air. The Drum Room was one of the few restaurants left in town that still allowed smoking.

Adam gestured toward one of the empty, lushly upholstered booths. "That okay?"

"Fine," Sawyer replied. He slid into the seat across from Adam, and a waiter immediately appeared at the booth.

"Two Scotches, top of the shelf," Adam said. "And bring us an order of those Cajun wings." Sawyer nodded to the waiter to let him know that was all.

Adam leaned back against the booth, looking inordinately pleased with himself. "I still can't believe we landed it. This is our ticket, Sawyer. This project will put us on the map, not just here in Baton Rouge, but all over the country."

He leaned forward, his gaze intense. "You've got to get all this legal crap behind you, Sawyer. I need your undivided attention on this. Ribideaux was quite impressed with your work."

Again Sawyer felt the tic along his jaw, the burn of the lighter inside his pocket. "I'm doing the best I can to get my legal issues behind me," he replied as calmly as possible. "I've retained Jackson Burdeaux in case things escalate."

Adam raised one of his blond eyebrows. "He's the best in the state. I certainly feel more comfortable knowing you have him on your side." He reached into his pocket and withdrew one of the Cuban cigars he was fond of. "Do you mind?" he asked as he tucked the cigar into the side of his mouth.

"Not at all." Sawyer reached into his pocket and pulled out the lighter. "Allow me." He flicked the flame to life.

"Hey!" Adam pulled the cigar from his mouth. "Where did you find my lighter? I've been looking for it for months."

At that moment the waiter arrived with their drinks and order. It wasn't until the waiter left that Adam again asked, "So where did you find it?"

Sawyer tucked the lighter back in his pocket. "I

found it in some of Erica's things." He stared at the man he'd considered a friend, as well as a partner. "When did you sleep with her, Adam? When did you have an affair with my wife?"

The fire of denial lit Adam's eyes as he met Sawyer's gaze. For a moment his mouth worked but nothing came out, then his eyes darkened and he stared down into his drink.

"It just happened once…about eight months ago." He looked at Sawyer, a deep agony darkening his eyes. "I'm sorry, Sawyer. God, I can't tell you how sorry I am. I hoped you'd never find out."

Adam leaned back once again and took a deep swallow of his drink. He stared off at some point just beyond Sawyer's shoulder. "She came to the office one day and you were out. She asked if she could sit in my office and wait for you. I poured her a drink, we chatted, and things just got out of control. Stella had been out of town for a week, Erica was coming on strong, and I had a weak moment."

Sawyer waited for the rage he'd expected to feel to fill him, but there was none. There was only a weary sadness that the people he'd thought he could rely on, the people he should have been able to trust, had betrayed him.

"It was just that once, Sawyer. I swear it was just that one time. Erica must have taken my lighter that day. I don't know why she'd do such a thing."

"I don't know why you'd do such a thing," Sawyer replied.

"Tell me how to fix it," Adam said fervently. "What can I do to make this right?"

"You've been talking about wanting to buy me out for months. Have your lawyer get in touch with me with a reasonable offer and I'm gone," Sawyer said.

"Jesus, Sawyer, that's not what I want, especially not now. Surely we can get past this. I've told you how sorry I am, how bad I feel about it."

"Adam, the problem is I can't get past it. The problem is now I understand that you have no integrity, and I can't work another day with a man who has no integrity."

Adam rubbed the center of his forehead, an anxious bewilderment twisting his features. "You can't mean that."

"But I do," Sawyer replied and stood. "And that's not the least of your problems. Now I have to turn this lighter over to Lucas Jamison and you'll be investigated as a potential suspect in Erica's murder." Adam's bewilderment transformed to horror.

"That's crazy," he exclaimed. "I had nothing to do with her death."

"You can tell it to the authorities. Enjoy your Cajun wings, Adam." With these words Sawyer turned and headed for the exit.

As he left the Drum Room and stepped out into the hot, sultry early-afternoon sun he hoped he hadn't just made a major mistake. He'd wanted to confront Adam, but he suddenly realized it was possible he'd just given Erica's murderer time to perfect an airtight alibi.

Chapter Nine

"I heard Sawyer quit his job," Lillian said as she and Amanda walked down the sidewalk toward Glad Rags, the absolutely most awesome boutique in town, according to Lillian.

It was Thursday midmorning and Sawyer had given her the morning off as he and Melanie had been invited to have brunch at a friend's home.

"Yeah, he went in Monday morning and told Adam he wanted out," Amanda replied.

"Why?" Lillian asked curiously. "Why would he want to quit his job?"

"He just decided maybe his time right now would be better spent at home with Melanie." It was the story Sawyer had come up with to tell people, even though he'd told Amanda what had really happened between him and Adam.

They had turned over the box of Erica's keepsakes to Lucas, and Amanda desperately hoped Lucas was doing his job and trying to find out who those items belonged to. It was quite possible that one of them was a murderer.

"Anything new in the investigation?" Lillian asked.

"No, nothing," Amanda replied. She could have told Lillian about finding the box, but she was tired of thinking about Erica's murder, tired of talking about it and speculating about it.

"What I'd really like to do is not think about all of it today," she said. "It seems like Erica's murder has consumed every minute of every day lately."

Lillian flashed her a bright smile and took her by the arm. "Then today it's strictly girlfriend fun. We'll buy something extravagant and useless, then go find someplace to have a decadent chocolate dessert."

Amanda laughed. "Sounds like a great plan."

Lillian hadn't exaggerated the pleasure of Glad Rags. The store sold not only darling blouses and skirts, jeans and dresses, but also offered a vast array of sexy lingerie and nightclothes.

The two women combed through the racks like excited teenagers, Amanda flipping through the jeans while Lillian beelined to a display of purses.

The saleslady, who introduced herself as Chloe, was friendly without being pushy. It was obvious Lillian was a frequent shopper as the two women chatted with an easy familiarity.

Amanda drifted from the jeans to the lingerie, eyeing the tiny colorful thongs and wispy bras. They were sexy and beautiful, but they were the kinds of things that had been in Erica's drawers and would never be found in hers.

She moved from the underwear display to the nightclothes. Red silk and black satin, lacy camisoles and tiny panties, so different from the nightshirts Amanda normally wore.

She ran her fingers over the short red silk nightgown. Closing her eyes, she imagined herself wearing it, a scarlet flame in the blacks and grays of Sawyer's bed.

"You're sleeping with him, aren't you?" Her eyes flew open and she stared at Lillian. Lillian laughed. "Don't try to deny it. I know that look you just had on your face."

Amanda felt as if her mother had just found out she was having premarital sex, and the feeling irritated her. "We're both adults. It's really nobody's business."

"Well of course it isn't," Lillian replied smoothly. She frowned slightly, the gesture forcing a line down the center of her forehead. "I just don't want you to get hurt, Amanda. I like you. I like you a lot. I don't want you to get your heart broken."

Amanda smiled at her warmly. "Don't worry, my heart is in no danger."

"Good." Lillian squeezed her arm, then wandered off toward another rack of clothing.

Amanda bought the nightgown, and Lillian bought a cute little pink shirt for Melanie and a new pair of slacks for herself.

After the dress shop they went to a nearby café and each of them ordered a cup of coffee and a piece of chocolate cake. "Melanie will love her new blouse," Amanda said as she cut into the dessert.

"I love to buy for her," Lillian replied.

"You're so good with her. Is there a reason you and James don't have children?" Amanda knew she was prying, but she was curious.

"We tried to get pregnant the first couple of years of our marriage. When it didn't happen each of us got checked out. The doctors couldn't find a reason why we couldn't, so we went home and tried some more. It just never happened for us."

She shrugged and picked up her coffee mug. "We talked about adopting, but by the time we thought about it, my art was taking up a lot of my time and James's insurance business was successful beyond our wildest dreams. We decided we liked our life as it was, just the two of us. What about you? You want kids?"

Amanda smiled. "I do. I love children. I'd like to have a couple of kids." She laughed. "Of course, a husband would be nice first."

Lillian took a sip of her coffee. "You're probably not going to find a husband being cooped up in Sawyer's house."

"I've got plenty of time to find a husband, have some kids and live happily ever after," Amanda replied lightly. She took a bite of her cake and tried not to think about how easy it would be to imagine she already had that, with Sawyer and Melanie.

"So what are your plans when your time with Melanie ends?" Lillian asked. "I mean, eventually either Sawyer will be in jail and other arrangements will have to be made for Melanie, or he won't go to jail and Melanie will eventually talk and she'll start back to school. Either way, your nanny job certainly isn't permanent."

"I knew it wasn't permanent when I took it, and I'm not sure what I'll do when it's over." The idea of returning to her old life certainly held no appeal.

"I hope you'll consider staying here in town," Lillian said. "I can't think of anyone else I'd rather go shopping or eat chocolate with."

Amanda laughed, warmed by the obvious friendship Lillian seemed to be offering. "I can't make any promises for the future," she said. "But I have to confess that Conja Creek is definitely working its magic on me."

Lillian's smile faded and she picked up her coffee cup and stared into the dark brew. "You know when I miss Erica the most?" Her smile was a soft, reflective, sad one. "About once a week late at night she'd call me and tell me to get my butt over to her dock. I'd walk over and meet her there and we'd sit in the dark and talk. Sometimes we just talked silly and laughed for half the night. Other times we'd talk about more serious things. I miss those nights."

She took a sip of her coffee, then lowered her cup back to the table. "Maybe some night we can get together on the dock and have a little girl talk in the darkness."

Amanda laughed. "I don't know, sounds kind of spooky to me."

"Ah, it's not spooky. It's kind of like being at camp. If you end up staying here in Conja Creek, then I think you're going to be my new camp buddy."

Later, as Amanda drove home, she thought about girlfriends she'd thought she'd had, friends who had distanced themselves when Amanda had found herself in trouble. It would be good to have a friend again, and Amanda suspected Lillian was a woman who wouldn't run at the first sign of problems.

It was true, Conja Creek had bewitched her. It wasn't just because of Sawyer and Melanie. Amanda liked the quaint charm of the town itself. Even the swamp drew her with its mysterious darkness.

Late this afternoon she and Sawyer were going to check out the motels whose matchbooks had been in Erica's things. Helen was watching Melanie, and Amanda fervently hoped she and Sawyer could discover something that would point a finger to the real guilty party.

Sawyer. A vision of him filled her head. Since the night they had made love there had been no more physical contact between them. Several times over the past couple of days Jackson Burdeaux had come to the house and the two men had holed up in Sawyer's office.

Jackson had told Sawyer that he was not to talk to Lucas anymore, that any and all communication between the sheriff and Sawyer would come through Jackson. Sawyer seemed fine with that.

It must be horrible to be unable to trust anyone in your life, she thought. She knew his discovery that Adam had slept with Erica had been an enormous blow even though he had downplayed it.

She parked her car in the driveway and got out, immediately stiffening as she saw George approaching her.

"Afternoon, Miss Nanny," he said.

"George." She nodded and headed toward the front door. He hurried after her and caught up to her just before she reached the porch.

He grabbed her by the arm. "I want to talk to you." He immediately dropped his hand back to his side. "Mr. Bennett told me I make you nervous. I just want you to know I had nothing to do with Erica's murder. I don't hurt pretty things."

"Okay," Amanda said, and backed away from him.

"I think it's a damn shame, what happened to Erica. But it wasn't me and you got to believe me. I've been working for Mr. Bennett for five years. I don't want no trouble, not from you or from anyone else. I mind my own business and you should do the same." Although there was no menace in his voice, his dark eyes shone with single-minded intent.

"Amanda?" Sawyer's voice came from the front

door and she breathed a sigh of relief. "I thought I heard your car. George, aren't you supposed to be weeding the back flower bed?"

"Yes, sir, I was just on my way there." George ambled away and Amanda hurried up the steps to where Sawyer awaited her.

"You okay?" he asked.

"Fine. He told me he didn't murder Erica."

Sawyer nodded. "George was one of the first people Lucas investigated. He has an airtight alibi for the night of Erica's murder." Sawyer ushered her through the front door. "That night George was at Cajun Country. He got drunk and passed out on the floor. The bartender let him sleep it off in the back room."

She followed him into the living room. "He's just a little bit creepy," she replied.

"He's odd," Sawyer agreed. "But if he's guilty of anything I suspect that he indulges in a little bit of illegal poaching."

"Then I guess that's one person I can mark off my suspect list," she replied.

He grinned at her, a slow easy smile that ignited a tiny flicker of warmth in her stomach. "You have a suspect list?"

"I do, and George is the first name I've been able to mark off."

"And who else is on your list?" He reached out and tucked a strand of her hair behind her ear. It was the first touch she'd had from him since the night they'd made love, and she willed herself not to ache for another from him.

"Everyone," she replied and stepped back from him. "Everyone I've met since I've arrived here."

"Am I on it?" His tone was light but there was suddenly an intense shine to his eyes, as if her answer was incredibly important to him.

"Sawyer, if your name was on the list, I wouldn't be here. I believe somebody killed your wife, viciously...horribly, but I'm positive that person wasn't you. And hopefully this afternoon, when we check out those motels, we'll be able to find out who Erica was seeing and who the real killer is."

"Have you always been an optimist?" he asked, his green eyes filled with the light of a man who wanted to believe.

"Always," she replied. Until those dark days following her resignation from her job, dark days when she'd lost her belief in anything good. But eventually the darkness had lifted and her natural belief in the goodness of people and life had returned.

"I have to believe that good wins, Sawyer. I have to believe that the guilty will be punished and you and Melanie will be able to get on with your lives."

"I hope you're right." He reached out and trailed a finger down her cheek. "I don't think I could have gotten through the past couple of weeks without you. You give me hope, Amanda."

It was at that moment Amanda realized she'd lied to Lillian. Her heart wasn't safe from this man;

it was intricately bound to his. She knew that eventually, when it came time to tell him goodbye, it would be one of the most difficult things she'd ever done in her life.

IT WAS JUST AFTER THREE when she and Sawyer got into his car to head to the motels they were going to check out. When they'd left, Melanie had been happily ensconced in the kitchen with Helen, helping to make dinner for that evening.

"Have you heard anything from Adam?" she asked once they were on the road.

"No, nothing," he replied. "I imagine he has his hands full. If Lucas has interviewed him, then Stella has probably found out about his fling with Erica, and she's not a woman who will easily forgive."

"Have you rethought your decision to walk away from your firm?"

"No. It's the right thing for me to do. I can't work with Adam anymore. I've lost all trust in him."

"Then what are you going to do?" she asked. "Eventually this will all be over and you'll have the rest of your life to think about."

He shot her a quick grin. "You mean what am I going to do if I don't end up making license plates for the rest of my life? I'll start over. I'll open my own office and continue to do what I enjoy doing, drawing plans for commercial buildings and homes."

They passed the rest of the drive in silence. The first motel they arrived at looked as if it had seen better days. The Night Owl had eight units housed in a low building that had weathered to a dull gray. The neon sign in the front blinked VAC N, as most of the bulbs were burned out.

"What possessed her?" Sawyer muttered under his breath as he pulled into a parking space in front of the office.

Amanda said nothing, but her thoughts mirrored his. What had possessed Erica to come here for a seedy affair? What demons had driven the woman to do the things she'd done? They would probably never know, but there was a small part of Amanda that was sad for the dead woman, who had apparently made bad choices that had led to her death.

"Let's get this over with," Sawyer said roughly and opened his car door.

Together they walked to the office, where the air smelled of stale body odors and a cheap pine cleaner. The man behind the counter looked up from a magazine he'd been reading as they approached.

"Help you?" he asked.

Sawyer withdrew his wallet and pulled out a picture of his late wife. "We were wondering if you'd seen this woman checking in with a particular man."

"Haven't seen her," the man said with barely a glance at the photo.

"I don't think you looked closely enough," Sawyer replied, his voice thrumming with suppressed energy.

Amanda pulled a twenty-dollar bill from her

purse and slid it across the counter, ignoring Sawyer's look of surprise. "Maybe you need to look again," she said.

The money disappeared quicker than a fly in the path of a frog's tongue. The man picked up the photo and studied it, then slid it back toward Sawyer and shook his head. "Never seen her before."

"Are you sure?" Amanda asked. She'd wanted answers, knew that Sawyer had wanted answers, as well. "Are you the only day clerk?"

"I'm the owner, and I'm on duty all the time. I haven't seen this woman. That doesn't mean she hasn't been here, that just means she wasn't the one who checked in." He reopened his magazine, dismissing them.

"That twenty-dollar bill was a pretty slick move," Sawyer said as they stepped back outside into the steaming sunshine.

"Yeah, well it always works in the movies, but it certainly didn't work for us," she replied.

"I owe you a twenty."

She flashed him a quick smile. "Consider it a donation to our cause."

"Maybe we'll have better results at the other places," Sawyer said when they were once again in his car and pulling away from the Night Owl.

Unfortunately the other three motels yielded the same results. None of the people staffing the front desks remembered seeing Erica.

Disappointment was the third passenger in the

car as they drove home. It sat in the silent space between them like a living, breathing entity.

Although Amanda desperately wanted to think of something to say that would make them both feel better, no words came to mind. What could you say to a man who was fighting for his life when every lead ended in a blind alley?

When they reached the house, Helen and Melanie had dinner waiting and the three of them sat down to a somber meal. Amanda picked at the pot roast with little appetite and noticed that Sawyer, too, didn't eat much.

It wasn't until after Melanie was asleep that she and Sawyer talked about the disappointment of the afternoon. She sat in the chair across from him as he leaned back in his desk-chair in his office.

"Maybe we're wasting our time, running around looking for a killer," he said. "Maybe it's nobody we know. It's possible Erica hooked up with somebody passing through town."

"Do you really believe that?"

He hesitated a long moment, then shook his head. "No, I don't. The only thing that makes sense is that the killer is somebody familiar with me, with Erica."

"And had something to lose if Erica went public with the affair," Amanda added. "Is it possible she could have been blackmailing somebody?"

He leaned forward and ran a hand down the side of his jaw. "I suppose anything is possible, but as crazy as it sounds, blackmail just doesn't seem like Erica's style."

"Maybe we should make a list of all the potential suspects and write down what their motive might be," she offered.

"That's a good idea." He booted up his computer and pulled up a Word file. She pulled her chair around the desk so she could sit next to him.

His cologne eddied in her head, for a moment making it difficult for her to focus. The heat of his body warmed her, and all she could think about was how it had felt to be held in his arms, how wonderful it had been when they'd made love.

"Lucas. He has to top the list," he said as he typed in the sheriff's name. "We know he had some kind of personal interaction with Erica."

"And as a close friend of yours, and being the sheriff, he wouldn't want an affair with her made public," she replied, forcing herself to focus on what they were doing. "Then there's Adam. Again, as your business partner and friend, he wouldn't want anyone to know he'd slept with Erica."

"And if that wasn't enough, there was the fact that he's married to Stella."

"Who else?" Amanda prompted.

He frowned and stared at the computer screen in front of him. "I suddenly realize how little I knew about how Erica spent her time while I was at work. I've always had a network of friends and business associates who occasionally came to the house, but none that she showed any real interest in."

"I've asked Lillian if she knew who Erica was having an affair with, but I didn't ask her if Erica showed any interest in anyone in particular. I'll ask her tomorrow."

"And I need to think, but at the moment my head is reeling and I can't seem to focus on anything." He saved the file, then punched off the computer. "I think I'll go for a walk, see if that clears my head."

"Then I'll just say good-night. It's been a long day." She moved the chair back where it belonged, then together they left his office.

She climbed the stairs as he went out the front door and into the night beyond. She went first to Melanie's room, comforted by the shine of the night-light and the soft, easy breaths of the sleeping child.

She stood at the doorway between the two bed-rooms and wondered what the future held for her, for Melanie and for Sawyer? How did a person investigate the last days or weeks of a woman's life when that woman had loved to keep secrets? If her best friend hadn't known who she was seeing or who might have interested her, then what hope did they have?

Turning away from Melanie's room, Amanda softly closed the bathroom door, then washed off her makeup, brushed her teeth and changed into the silk nightgown she'd bought that morning.

As the silk slid down her body to her knees, she told herself she'd bought the gown for herself, not for Sawyer, but she couldn't help but imagine how his hands would warm the cool material.

She left the bathroom and went directly to her bedroom window, peering outside to see if she'd catch a glimpse of Sawyer walking the grounds. There was nobody there, only the ghostly shadows of the trees and tall brush against the silvery moonlight.

Getting into bed, she tried to shove all thoughts of Sawyer and murder out of her head. Tomorrow she and Melanie would spend the day doing something fun, something that would keep her mind off everything else.

Maybe she'd been spending too much time doing all the things that weren't in her job description and not enough time working with Melanie. Maybe a little art therapy would help unlock Melanie. Yes, they'd spend the day drawing, she thought with certainty.

Minutes ticked by and suddenly all she could think about was the leftover ham from the night before that was in the refrigerator. She'd only picked at dinner and now her stomach rumbled with pangs that she knew would probably keep her from sleeping.

She got back out of bed and pulled on her robe, then headed for the stairs. The downstairs was dark, and she didn't know if Sawyer had come back from his walk yet or not.

She didn't turn on any lights, familiarity making it easy for her to navigate her way across the living room and into the kitchen.

The refrigerator light flashed on as she opened the door, and she immediately spied the ham wrapped in cellophane. Just a few pieces, she told herself as she pulled the ham from the fridge and placed it on the countertop.

She had just unwrapped it when she heard something…an indistinguishable noise. She froze for a moment, then turned around. "Sawyer?" she whispered softly.

She waited for an answering reply, but there was none, nor did she hear the sound again. She turned back to the ham and picked off several slices.

The noise again. A rustling. Was that a faint footstep? She whirled around, the hairs on the nape of her neck rising. Nothing. Holding her breath, she listened but there was nothing to hear.

An overactive imagination, she told herself. And surely under the circumstances she was allowed a little flirting with jumpiness.

She picked up the platter of ham and opened the fridge door to return it to the shelf. A noise sounded behind her, and the air around her was suddenly displaced. She dropped the ham, the platter crashing to the floor as she started to turn to see who was in the room with her.

Before she could see who was behind her, something crashed into the back of her head and the floor rose up to greet her.

Chapter Ten

Sawyer walked the grounds of his estate, needing to work off the restless energy that pulsed in his veins. The energy was one part frustration and one part desire, the combination making him wonder if he was losing his mind.

As he'd tried to type in a list of potential suspects, all he'd really wanted to do was lose himself in Amanda. In her arms he knew he could find escape from his reality.

He was confused about his feelings for her, and in any case was wary of exploring them. At the moment he felt as if he had no future. He was having difficulty looking beyond the next minute.

He wound up on the dock where the moonlight found it impossible to pierce through the thick trees. He'd held on to Erica too long, unwilling to admit failure, hoping she'd change for Melanie's sake.

"I should have let her go," he murmured. He should have divorced her, given her a big settlement then shoved her out the door. If he'd done that, she would probably be alive today.

Funny, he hadn't loved her, and even though he'd known deep in his heart she was running around on him, he hadn't hated her, either. There had been flashes of goodness in her, but they'd often been overwhelmed by whatever demons rode her soul.

And now she was gone and Sawyer was in trouble and he didn't know how to help himself. Jackson had assured him that he wouldn't spend a day in jail, but that was Jackson's job as a defense attorney, to reassure his client.

There was no way that he'd believe the killer wasn't somebody he knew, somebody who lived in Conja Creek, who'd been to his home before.

The restless energy that had burned through him dissipated, leaving him exhausted. Time to call it a night. He turned to face the house, and at that moment a scream ripped through the night.

His heart constricted and he ran toward the house as the scream came again. Melanie. The distance between the dock and the house suddenly seemed like miles as he raced across it, the screams coming one after another in rapid succession.

These weren't like her usual nightmare screams. These held a horror that echoed back to the past, back to the night that Erica had been murdered.

He burst through the back doors and immediately realized the screams weren't coming from Melanie's bedroom, but rather from the kitchen.

He ran into the kitchen and stopped in the doorway, for a moment the scene before him not making any sense. Amanda lay on the floor in front of the refrigerator, and Melanie stood next to her, eyes wide as another scream ripped from her throat.

For a moment he was frozen as his brain tried to work around a scenario that would make sense. The inertia broke as he saw the dark stain of blood matting the back of Amanda's head. Oh, God, she looked as if she was dead.

He knelt down beside her, at the same time gathering Melanie against him with one arm. "It was the swamp monster," Melanie cried. "I know it was the swamp monster who hurt Amanda."

"Shh, it's all right now, baby. Daddy's here." Sawyer moved the hair from Amanda's neck and checked her pulse. Thank God there was a pulse.

He needed a phone and his gun. He didn't know if anyone was in the house or not. He had a hysterical eight-year-old in one arm and a comatose woman with an apparent head wound on the floor. He needed help.

Although he hated to leave Amanda where she was, he wanted his gun in his hand, wanted something standing between him and the "swamp monster," as Melanie had said.

With Melanie in his arms he raced through the living room and into his office, flipping on lights as he went so there were no shadows in which to hide.

It took him only a minute to unlock the drawer that

contained his gun. He laid the gun on the desk, called 911 and told the operator he needed the sheriff and an ambulance, gave her his address, then hung up.

As he left the office, gun in one hand, Melanie in the other, she clung to him like a tick, her legs wrapped tightly around him and her hands clutched around his neck. She wasn't screaming anymore, nor did she say a word, but her terror communicated itself through the frantic trembling that suffused her body.

They returned to the kitchen where Amanda hadn't moved. He sat on the floor next to her, Melanie in his lap. He reached out and moved a strand of hair from Amanda's face. Her eyelids fluttered but didn't open.

"Amanda, wake up," Melanie said, her voice a childish plea that ripped at Sawyer's heart. "Please wake up. I'm scared."

Again Amanda's eyelids fluttered and this time opened. For a moment she stared at them, obviously disoriented. "Oh," the word whispered out of her, and she winced and struggled to sit up.

"No, don't," Sawyer said. Relief loosened the cold, hard knot that had been in his chest. He reached out and gently pushed her back to the floor. "Just lie still until the ambulance gets here."

"Ambulance?" She repeated the word as if she'd never heard it before. "I don't need an ambulance." She winced again and reached up to touch the back of her head. When she saw her bloodied hand she forced a smile that more resembled a grimace. "Okay, maybe an ambulance isn't such a bad idea after all."

Her stab at humor did more to ease his worry that anything else could have. Still, the wound on the back of her head scared the hell out of him, and he had no idea what had happened and didn't want to ask too many questions with Melanie sitting on his lap, obviously still frightened.

"Melanie, sweetie, I'm okay, so don't look so sad," Amanda said. Once again she struggled to sit up, refusing Sawyer's attempt to keep her down. "I just bumped my head too hard, that's all."

Melanie bit her bottom lip as tears welled up in her eyes. Sawyer tightened his arm around his daughter. "It was the swamp monster," she said, her voice barely above a whisper. "I saw it. The monster hit Amanda."

"What do you mean, honey? What swamp monster?" Sawyer asked.

"The same one who killed Mommy. I saw the monster in the kitchen. It hit Amanda then it ran past me and out the front door." Melanie hid her face in the front of Sawyer's shirt. "I'm afraid, Daddy. I'm afraid."

"There's nothing to be afraid of," Sawyer assured her. "Daddy would never let a swamp monster hurt you." He exchanged a confused glance with Amanda. Had Melanie really seen somebody in the house? Or was this just the hysterical imagining of a little girl who had already been traumatized?

Had somebody hit Amanda over the head or had she somehow tripped and smashed her head against the refrigerator or against the floor?

"Sawyer?"

Lucas Jamison's voice came from the front door. "In the kitchen," Sawyer called back.

Lucas entered with his gun drawn, followed by Maria Kelso, a female deputy and two EMTs. When he saw the three of them on the floor, he holstered his gun and motioned for the two EMTs to attend to Amanda.

"What happened?"

"I'm not sure, but I think it's possible somebody came into the house."

Instantly Lucas's gun was back in his hand. "You know how to use that?" he gestured toward Sawyer's gun.

"I do," Sawyer replied.

"Maria, let's clear the house." Together they left the room. Sawyer watched as the EMTs began to check out Amanda. As one of them looked at her head wound, the other placed a blood pressure cuff around her upper arm.

"Do you know what day it is?" The one who looked at her head asked.

"It's Thursday night," she replied.

"And what's your name?"

"Amanda Rockport. I'm fine, really. My head hurts, but other than that I'm okay." As the blood pressure cuff came off, she pulled her robe more closely around her.

Sawyer stood, Melanie still clinging to him like a frightened monkey. The EMT with the name tag reading Ben held out a hand to Amanda. "Let's get you off the floor."

They helped her up, and by the time she was in a kitchen chair and they had finished checking her out, Maria and Lucas returned to the kitchen. Sawyer placed his gun in a kitchen drawer and joined them at the table.

"House is clear," Lucas said tersely. "Amanda, how are you doing?"

"I have a headache and I feel a little woozy, but other than that I'm all right."

"She might have a mild concussion," Ben said. "The head wound looks worse than it is. Head wounds always look bad because they bleed so much."

"Okay, so somebody want to tell me what happened?" Lucas asked.

"Maybe Maria would like to take Melanie into the living room," Sawyer suggested pointedly. The last thing he wanted was to further upset her, although he knew eventually that Lucas would want to talk to her. However at this point, Sawyer didn't know if she would speak again.

He rubbed down Melanie's back. "Sweetie, why don't you go with Maria and let the grown-ups talk for a few minutes." Maria had a daughter who was in Melanie's class at school. Melanie had been to Maria's house before and so knew the woman well enough to not be afraid.

Reluctantly she slid off Sawyer's lap and took the hand Maria proffered. "Come on, honey. The joy of having cable television is no matter what time it is there are cartoons on."

When they had left the room, Amanda looked at the two EMTs. "You can go. I'll be all right."

"It wouldn't hurt for you to go to the hospital and get checked more thoroughly," Ben said.

"No, I'm fine."

Lucas nodded to dismiss them. When they, too, had left the room, he looked at Amanda expectantly. "What happened?"

Now that some of the adrenaline of the past few minutes was passing Sawyer wanted to take her in his arms, ease the painful wince of her eyes, the faint darkness that resided there.

"I went to bed but I got hungry. I remembered there was some leftover ham in the refrigerator." She looked stricken and glanced over to the floor where the broken platter of ham remained on the floor. "I dropped it, I'm so sorry," she said to Sawyer.

"To hell with the ham," he replied roughly.

She frowned. "I heard something. I'm not sure what it was, a faint rustle, a footstep…something that didn't sound right. I turned but couldn't see anything or anyone. I thought it was just my imagination. I got my ham and was about to put the remainder of it back into the refrigerator when I knew I wasn't alone in the kitchen. I started to turn around to see who was there, but I got slammed in the back of the head and that's all I know."

A slow rage began to build in Sawyer. Somebody

had come into his home. Somebody had attacked Amanda in his kitchen. Guilt tempered the rage. He hadn't bothered to lock up the house when he'd gone for his walk. He'd always felt safe here, had never bothered much with the security system or locking the doors when he was home.

"Melanie found her," he now said. "Melanie said it was a swamp monster, the same monster who killed Erica."

One of Lucas's dark eyebrows shot up. "Melanie is talking?"

"She did tonight," Sawyer replied. His heart swelled. She'd talked. Not just a word, not just two, but really talked. "She said that the swamp monster ran past her and left through the front door."

"I'll need to talk to her," Lucas said. Sawyer nodded and Lucas turned his attention back to Amanda. "Have you had any problems with anyone in the past couple of days? Any words exchanged or issues?"

"No, nothing," she replied. Some of the color had returned to her face. "I can't imagine why anyone would want to hurt me."

"And you didn't get a look at the person? Nothing that could help us identify your attacker?" Lucas asked.

Helplessly she shook her head, her lips pressed together as if in pain. "I don't have a clue who it might have been," she finally said.

"Let's get Melanie back in here, see if she can tell

us anything that will help," Lucas said. He called to Maria, who brought Melanie back into the kitchen. To Sawyer's surprise, instead of coming to him, she went to Amanda and got up in her lap. Amanda's arms wound around her, lovingly, protectively.

"Melanie, we need you to tell Lucas what you saw tonight," Sawyer said gently.

Melanie turned her face into the front of Amanda's robe. "Melanie, honey, somebody tried to hurt me tonight and we need to know what you saw or heard so we can put the bad person in jail," Amanda said.

Melanie looked up at her, then at Sawyer. Finally she looked at Lucas, as if assessing if it would be safe to talk to him. "It was the swamp monster," she said, her voice barely audible.

"The swamp monster?" Lucas looked at Sawyer, then back at Melanie.

"The swamp monster that killed Mommy."

"And what did the swamp monster look like?" Lucas sat up straighter in the kitchen chair.

"I couldn't see good. It was dark, but the swamp monster is dark and scary and kills people." Melanie's voice trembled, and Sawyer saw Amanda's arms tighten around her. "And it smells bad."

"Smells bad? Like what?" Sawyer asked.

"It smells icky. I smelled it when it ran by me."

"But how does icky smell?" Lucas asked, obviously wanting her to be more specific.

"It smells like a swamp monster," Melanie replied. Although Lucas wanted more from her, it was equally obvious that they were going in circles.

"Why did you come downstairs?" Sawyer asked his daughter gently.

"I woke up and Amanda wasn't in her bed so I came downstairs looking for her." Once again she turned her head and buried her face in Amanda's robe.

"Melanie, can you tell me what you saw the night your mother died?" Lucas asked.

"The swamp monster stabbed mommy, then pushed her off the dock."

"And could you see what the monster looked like that night?" Lucas asked.

"Big and dark and scary." Her voice was just a bare whisper and she trembled in Amanda's arms.

"Could you see the monster's face?" Lucas leaned forward.

Melanie shook her head. "But I know it was ugly and bad."

They weren't going to get the answers they needed from Melanie. Sawyer had no idea what she'd really seen the night that Erica had been murdered or tonight with Amanda, but it was obvious that in her little-girl mind the culprit was a faceless, frightening monster.

"I'll check around the outside of the house, see if I can find any evidence of an intruder," Lucas said, apparently coming to the same conclusion as Sawyer.

"I'll go out with you," Sawyer said and stood. He looked at Amanda. "Will you be okay?"

"We're fine," she assured him. "I think maybe we'll go back into the living room and watch some more cartoons. How does that sound, Melanie?"

Melanie nodded and got up from Amanda's lap. They all left the kitchen and when they reached the living room Amanda sat on the sofa and Melanie stretched out with her head in Amanda's lap.

Sawyer, Lucas and Maria stepped out on the front porch. "Maria, why don't you go around back and check things out," Lucas instructed.

When she'd disappeared around the corner of the house, Lucas turned back to Sawyer. "I know where Amanda and Melanie were in all this. What I don't know is where you were while Amanda was being attacked in the kitchen." There was no hint of friendship coming from Lucas. He was all business, and anything the two men might have shared in the past was only a distant memory.

"I'd gone for a walk."

Lucas raised an eyebrow. "Outside? In the middle of the night?"

"It wasn't exactly the middle of the night," Sawyer replied. "And I needed to clear my head."

"So Amanda didn't know where you were when she got hit over the head." Lucas's voice was flat, emotionless.

Sawyer narrowed his eyes. "Are you implying something?" Was it possible Lucas thought he was the swamp monster? That he'd sneaked up behind Amanda and smashed her in the back of the head?

"I'll tell you what's odd, that the attacker ran past Melanie without apparent concern that she might identify him. I find it damned odd that Amanda was attacked and Melanie was left untouched."

"What do you think, Lucas? That I pretended to go outside for a walk, but instead waited for Amanda to get hungry, then attacked her?" His voice sounded uneven, stressed, even to his own ears. "Melanie was standing there, but of course I didn't want to hurt my daughter, so I ran past her in the dark. Then I called you so that you could be here to investigate. Does that make sense to you?"

"None of this makes sense," Lucas replied. His gaze remained intent on Sawyer. "All I know for sure is that the women beneath your roof don't seem to fare too well."

MELANIE HAD FALLEN ASLEEP in her lap. Amanda remained seated, stroking her hair and fighting the worst headache she'd ever had in her life.

Somebody had attacked her. Somebody had hit her over the head with enough force to knock her unconscious. Who had been in the house and why had she been a target?

What frightened her more than anything were the what-ifs that played in her mind. What if Melanie hadn't awakened at that moment and shown up in the kitchen when she had? Would the attacker have struck Amanda again?

And again?

Until there was no more life in her?

Had Melanie inadvertently stopped a murder? Despite the warmth of the house, a cold chill stalked up her spine. Why would anyone want her dead? There was nothing to be gained by her death. She closed her eyes, fighting the pain in her head, the fear in her soul.

Her eyes flew open as she heard the sound of the front door opening, then closing. A moment later Sawyer came in, his features taut with stress.

"Did you find anything?" she asked softly.

"No, nothing. The ground is too hard to show any footsteps, and whoever it was left nothing behind. Of course, Lucas thinks I might be responsible."

She stared at him in disbelief. "For hitting me? That's utterly ridiculous," she scoffed.

He sat in one of the chairs opposite the sofa. "He thinks it's odd that Melanie wasn't hurt."

Amanda stroked Melanie's hair once again. "I think she saved my life. I think whoever attacked me didn't intend to stop with that one blow, and if Melanie hadn't shown up in the kitchen and screamed, I wouldn't be here to talk to you now."

He stood and gestured toward the sleeping child. "I'll carry her up to bed, then we can talk." He walked over and lifted Melanie as if she weighed no more than a feather. She didn't stir from her sleep as he gathered her in his arms and headed for the stairs.

Remembering the broken platter and ham still on

the floor in the kitchen, she got up from the sofa, intent on cleaning up the mess that had been made. After the mess was cleaned up she definitely needed to find a couple of aspirins and see she if could get a handle on the pounding in her head.

She was bent over picking up the last of the pieces of the platter when Sawyer returned. "You don't have to do that," he protested.

"I made the mess, I'll clean it up. At least the platter didn't shatter, but I'm afraid the ham is a total loss." Tears burned in her eyes as suppressed emotions suddenly rose up in her chest.

"Amanda."

His gentle voice made the tears burn hotter. He grabbed her to him and wrapped his arms around her. She stood in the embrace, shivering as tears raced down her cheeks.

"You're all right now," he said softly. "You're safe and we'll make sure that you stay safe."

She laughed self-consciously and swiped at her cheeks. "I'm sorry. I don't know why I'm crying." She made no move to step away from him, needed the warmth and strength of his strong arms surrounding her as the full realization of what had just happened swept through her. She buried her face in the front of his shirt, smelling the mixture of his cologne and the wild scent of night that clung to him.

"I'd say you deserve a good cry," he replied. "You've just been through a terrifying experience."

She raised her face to look at him. "Why would somebody want to hurt me?"

He dropped his arms from around her and motioned to the chairs at the table. "I don't know." His voice radiated with his frustration. "Maybe we stirred somebody up by going to those motels and asking questions."

"But we didn't get any answers," she replied. "How could we have made somebody nervous? And that still doesn't answer why somebody would want to get to me."

"It's all my fault." He gazed at her intently. "Dammit, it's all my fault. I walked out of here without locking the doors, without setting the security alarm." He muttered a curse.

"Sawyer, you can't blame yourself," she protested. "Who would have thought that somebody would have the nerve to creep into a house where we were all home?"

"I don't know. All I do know is that from now on the doors are locked at all times and the security system is on. We both have to be vigilant whenever we leave the house and when we're here."

She leaned back in the chair. "You don't have any old girlfriends who might have whacked me over the head because of some jealousy issue, do you?"

"Absolutely not. Unlike Erica, I took my marriage vows very seriously. There're no old girlfriends in my past."

"What about Helen?"

He sat back in surprise. "I sure haven't ever entertained any romantic thoughts about Helen."

She couldn't help the brief burst of laughter that left her lips. He looked so appalled at the very thought. The laughter was short-lived. "I mean, what about Helen as a murder suspect?"

"You've got to be kidding," he said with more than a touch of disbelief.

She leaned forward and tried to ignore the pounding of her head. "Think about it, Sawyer. She hasn't hidden the fact that she hated Erica, that she thought Erica was all wrong for you and Melanie.

"But she's an old woman. Surely she couldn't have overwhelmed Erica with her physical strength," he protested.

"Have you seen her rolling out bread dough or hacking up a chicken? She has more strength in her arms than I'll ever have, especially if she was driven by hate."

Sawyer rubbed two fingers in the center of his forehead, as if he could feel the pounding of her head in his own. "Then why would Helen want to hurt you? I thought the two of you were getting along just fine."

"I thought we were, too. But that would certainly explain why Melanie wasn't hurt. I think Helen loves her more than anything or anyone else on earth."

"Helen has worked for me and my family for years and I've never seen any indication that she's capable of violence." He sighed wearily. "We're not going to solve this tonight." He eyed her sympathetically. "How's your head?"

"On a scale of one to ten, ten being the worst pain I've ever had, this is about a twenty." She reached up and touched the back of her head where dried blood caked her hair. The paramedics had washed out the wound with peroxide but hadn't removed all the blood. "I guess I'm due a hair washing before I call it a night. I don't want to get into bed with this blood in my hair."

"Why don't you let me help? We could wash it right here in the kitchen sink."

She had never considered allowing a man to help her wash her hair, but she'd never been hit in the head from behind, either. At the moment his offer sounded incredibly appealing. "I'll go get a towel and my shampoo."

As she climbed each step to her bedroom, her head pounded and the questions that had plagued her since she'd regained consciousness stabbed in her brain.

Had the attacker watched the house and when Sawyer went for his walk saw an opportunity to strike? But why her? What would anyone have to gain by killing her?

Who was Melanie's swamp monster? And how many victims would the monster claim before finally being caught?

Chapter Eleven

Amanda awoke late the next morning. She knew it was late by the bright sunshine that poured through her window. She rolled over on her side and gazed at the clock on her nightstand. Ten o'clock! She couldn't remember the last time she'd overslept like this.

She shot straight up, and the dull throb in her head sent all the events of the previous night back. Although her head ached, it wasn't the sharp, nauseating pain of the night before. She slid from the bed and checked Melanie's room, not surprised to find it empty.

If she were to guess, there had been a conspiracy between Sawyer and Melanie to let her sleep in. She was thankful. After the horror of the night before, she'd needed the extra rest.

She dressed quickly, and as she stood in front of the bathroom mirror and brushed her hair she remembered the tenderness of Sawyer as he'd washed her hair in the kitchen sink.

She'd never known a man like him before, a man who exhibited such inner strength, such a command of the air around him and yet enough tenderness to bring tears to her eyes.

He'd combed out her hair, found her a couple of aspirins, then had walked her to her bedroom door and sent her off to bed with a kiss on the forehead.

She turned away from the mirror, not wanting to see in her eyes what she knew was in her heart for Sawyer. Despite all her desire to the contrary, she was more than half in love with the man, a man who might not have a future.

As she went down the stairs, the only sound, a rattling of dishes, came from the kitchen. She walked in to see Helen unloading the dishwasher.

For a moment Helen seemed unaware of her presence, and Amanda took the opportunity to watch her. Sawyer had pooh-poohed Amanda's suspicions of the older woman, but Amanda still wondered if she'd harbored enough hatred in her heart to kill Erica.

Of course, that didn't answer the question of why Helen might have attacked Amanda. Unless Helen wanted to be the only woman in the Bennett home, unless Helen wanted to be the only woman in Melanie's life.

"You going to stand there staring all morning or are you going to come in and sit down?" Helen said without turning around to look at her.

A blush warmed Amanda's cheeks. "I'm going

"She was talking this morning?"

"Chattering like a magpie," Helen replied, and all her features softened as she spoke of Melanie. "Music to my ears, it was, after all those days of silence."

"I'm glad. I was afraid that she'd only talked last night because of the dramatic circumstances." Amanda's heart rejoiced at the news that Melanie was finally really talking.

She was just about to head up the stairs to her bedroom when she heard a knock on the front door. "I'll get it," she called to Helen, then peered through the peephole in the door to see James standing on the front porch.

She opened the door. "Hi, James," she greeted him as she gestured him into the entry.

"Amanda." He offered her a friendly smile as he pulled a handkerchief out of his pocket and swiped at his gleaming forehead. "Not even noon yet and already it's hot as Hades."

"It is warm. If you're here looking for Sawyer, I'm afraid he's not home," she said.

"Actually, I'm looking for my lovely wife. Her car was at home but I couldn't find her anywhere on the premises. I thought maybe she'd walked over here to have coffee with you."

"No, I'm sorry but I haven't seen her this morning."

"Ah, well it was worth a try. You know she thinks a lot of you."

"I like her, too," Amanda replied. "She's really the only woman I know here in town."

He smiled. "She'll run you ragged if you let her. Shopping and lunch with her friends, that's what my Lilly loves. I guess I'll head back home and hunt some more. She can't have gone too far." He stepped back out the front door. "Nice seeing you again, Amanda." With a wave he walked off the porch and back toward his car.

Amanda closed the front door and relocked it, then went upstairs to her bedroom. She felt a sudden need to connect with her brother. She'd spoken to him several times since being here, but hadn't talked to him for a little over a week.

Unfortunately all she got when she called was his voice mail. She didn't leave a message, for at that moment she heard the front door open then close.

"Amanda, come see what Daddy got for me." Melanie's voice sailed up the stairs. Unexpected emotion crawled up her throat as she heard the happiness in Melanie's sweet voice. She'd heard it tinged with desperation on the night Sawyer had told Amanda to leave. Last night she'd heard it filled with terror as she'd talked about the swamp monster. But now Melanie's voice sang the way little-girl voices were supposed to, with excitement and joy.

"Come on, Amanda. Hurry!" Melanie squealed and giggled and Sawyer's deep laughter added appealing contrast. Amanda hurried down the stairs to the living room, where Sawyer sat on the sofa and Melanie was in the middle of the floor being licked half to death by a black-and-white furball of a puppy.

"Oh my," Amanda said in surprise.

"His name is Buddy 'cause Daddy said I needed a snuggle buddy for when I'm scared or sad," Melanie exclaimed.

"I know dog trainer isn't exactly in your job description," Sawyer began.

Amanda held up a hand to stop him. "Please, I threw out the job description a long time ago."

"He has his own crate in the utility room and I've explained to Melanie that Buddy will sleep there until he's old enough to understand the rules," Sawyer said.

Melanie picked up the wiggling ball of fur. "He's gonna learn the rules real fast 'cause I can tell he's really, really smart."

"Why don't you take him to the utility room to show him where he's going to stay," Sawyer suggested.

She stood and giggled again as Buddy lavished her neck and cheeks with puppy kisses. It was only when she'd left the room that Sawyer looked at Amanda and all trace of laughter fell from his features.

"I had some paperwork to drop off at Jackson Burdeaux's this morning," he said. "And while I was there Lucas called him."

She knew the news was bad, knew by the bleakness of his dark green eyes, the deep line that cut across his forehead as he frowned. She steeled herself for what he was about to tell her. "And what did Lucas want?" she asked.

"To tell Jackson that an arrest warrant has been issued for me."

She gasped and closed her eyes against the bitter disappointment and fear his words invoked. They had both known that this was a possibility, but she'd hoped for a break in the case that would keep this from happening. She opened her eyes and gazed at him. "So, what happens now?"

"Lucas has extended me the courtesy of turning myself in at the station with Jackson first thing tomorrow morning. He thought it would be less traumatic for everyone involved."

"Less traumatic? How can any of this be less traumatic?" she replied.

"It beats being led away from my home in handcuffs," he replied drily.

The vision of him in handcuffs shot a rivulet of pain through her. "This wasn't supposed to happen," she said angrily, bitterly. "The guilty person should be going to jail, not you."

"Took the words right out of my mouth." He smiled, but it was a forced, empty gesture. "The bad news is I won't be arraigned until Monday morning. The good news is Jackson feels confident I'll be able to bail out."

"On a murder charge?"

"I have long-standing ties to the community. I'm a respected businessman and I have a daughter without a parent. Jackson seems to think all of that will work in my favor when it comes to the judge setting bail."

"If he's right, then you could be home Monday afternoon."

He nodded and for a moment gazed at a spot just over her shoulder. She knew what he was thinking, the same thing she was thinking. If Jackson was wrong, then it was possible he might never come home again.

SAWYER WATCHED MELANIE running in the front yard with her new puppy. Amanda sat next to him on the porch steps. He'd told her he wanted to spend the day with her and Melanie, doing ordinary things and just enjoying the sunshine and whatever laughter they could find.

"I'm not making any permanent arrangements for Melanie or anything else at the moment," he said, breaking the silence that had descended between him and Amanda. "If the worst happens and I'm not home on Monday, I can figure things out then. But no matter what, I'd like you to consider staying on." Her soft-blue eyes gazed at him in surprise. "I'll double your salary," he exclaimed. "I'll triple it if you want me to."

She smiled, a sad gesture that deepened the blue of her eyes. "The money isn't important." She looked back at Melanie. "I just want to do whatever is best for her."

"And that's why I want you here." He reached for her hand and took it in his. "She loves you, Amanda. More importantly, she trusts you."

She squeezed his hand. "And I love her."

"If I don't come home, if the worst thing happens, then I've already set up a trust. You and Melanie could remain in the house and you could raise her like she's your own."

Her pained expression made him realize how preposterous the idea was. Why would a pretty young woman with her whole life ahead of her want to bind herself to such an arrangement? "Never mind, it was a stupid idea."

"No, it's not, it's just that there are things you need to know about me, about what brought me here." The darkness of her eyes grew more intense and she pulled her hand from his.

"Amanda, there's nothing I need to know other than that you love my daughter. When I think of her sick and crying, if I can't be here to comfort her, then you're my next choice. I know you have a beautiful heart and soul, and that's all I care about."

She started to say something but at that moment Melanie came running toward them, Buddy wiggling in her arms. "He told me he's tired of running," she said, half out of breath.

As he looked at his daughter, Sawyer's heart swelled up in his chest, and for a moment the emotion was so thick he couldn't speak, he could scarcely breathe.

"Maybe what Buddy needs is a big drink of water and a short nap," Amanda said. "Why don't we take him inside."

"You two go ahead," Sawyer managed to say.

"Come on, sweetie," Amanda said to Melanie. "I think I could use something cold to drink, too."

As they disappeared into the house, Sawyer drew in a deep breath, wanting, needing to gain control of his emotions.

Melanie was only eight. If things went badly she'd be a middle-aged woman when he eventually got out of prison. For all intents and purposes he would miss the most important years of her life.

As he stared out across the expanse of lawn, the trees became nothing more than watery green-blues. He hadn't shed a tear when Erica had died. He hadn't even cried when Melanie had gone mute. But the idea of losing Melanie's childhood, of being absent for her first date and prom and all the other experiences she'd have, crushed his soul and he couldn't stanch the tears that trekked down his cheeks.

He closed his eyes and focused on the items he'd turned over to Lucas. Erica's souvenirs. The gold lighter belonged to Adam. Adam was an unfaithful husband, a friend who'd betrayed, but according to Lucas, Adam wasn't a killer. The night Erica had been murdered, Adam and his wife had attended a dinner party with several other couples.

He thought of the picture frame with the embossed roses and hearts. He'd seen it someplace before, but for the life of him he couldn't remember where. The other items he was relatively sure he'd never seen before.

He still wasn't sure about Lucas's culpability, and his uncertainty about his friend ripped the very guts out of him. He and Lucas had always been close, but this case and suspicion of each other had fractured their friendship.

Standing up from the steps, he realized he needed to go back inside. He wanted to spend every moment that he could with Melanie. Thank God he wasn't arrested before she'd found her voice again. At least he'd be able to hear her little voice in his head as the sound of the jail cell door clanged shut behind him.

Chapter Twelve

You have to tell him. The little voice inside Amanda's head whispered those words throughout the rest of the day, as they ate dinner and now as she stood in Melanie's doorway and watched Sawyer kiss his daughter good-night.

He has a right to know. She couldn't agree to being here permanently with Melanie without telling Sawyer about the tragic events that had brought her here.

She focused on Sawyer, seated on the edge of Melanie's bed. He'd be gone tomorrow, and none of them knew what the future held. Her heart squeezed painfully at the very thought of his absence.

They'd spent some time this evening going over things while Melanie was playing with Buddy. It would just be Amanda and Melanie in the house for the next couple of days. Knowing that everyone was a potential suspect, he'd given Helen and George two weeks off. He'd reminded Amanda to be sure and use the security system and had done everything he possibly could to ensure their safety while he was gone.

They both were functioning on the premise that he would be home on Monday. Any other scenario was impossible to imagine.

As Sawyer kissed Melanie's forehead, Amanda's heart constricted anew. He'd told his daughter that he was going away for a couple of days, but Amanda knew he had to be wondering if the kiss he'd just placed on Melanie's forehead would be his last.

When he rose from the bed no emotion rode his features. It was as if he'd taken himself to a place where nothing could reach him, nothing could hurt him.

He motioned her to follow him out to the hall. "How about a drink?"

"I'll be down in just a minute," she said. "And then we need to talk."

He nodded and headed for the stairs as Amanda went to her bedroom. Once there she went to the closet and pulled out her suitcase. She'd unpacked everything when she'd first arrived, everything but one item. She opened the case and withdrew the newspaper that was inside.

Sitting on the side of her bed, she opened it, and as always the headline punched her in the gut with a blow strong enough to make her sick. School Counselor or Girlfriend? Did Inappropriate Personal Relationship Drive Student to Suicide?

She closed her eyes, but the words had long ago been burned into her brain. That headline had been the beginning of the worst three weeks of her life she'd believed she would ever endure. And now she needed to share that agonizing event with Sawyer.

Her feet felt leaden as she walked down the stairs and headed for his office where she knew he'd be seated behind his desk, a glass of Scotch in hand.

He smiled as she entered the room, a tired smile that hinted at the emotional exhaustion he obviously felt. She wished she could make it better for him, but she was afraid what she was going to tell him would only make things worse. She realized her timing was terrible, but it couldn't be helped.

"Now what was it that you wanted to tell me?" he asked.

In answer she handed him the newspaper and watched his eyes widen slightly as he saw the headline. As he read the accompanying article, she tried to read his features, but his face was expressionless.

The article was the worst kind of journalism, slanted with veiled accusations for the maximum exploitative punch. "Okay, I've read it, now you want to tell me what happened?" He tossed the paper aside as if it were no more than a piece of trash.

She sank onto the chair opposite him and floundered as to where to begin. "His name was Bobby Miller. He was a troubled fourteen-year-old. I was meeting with him once a week at school to talk about things…you know, his class work, his attitude toward school and his fellow students. He had a bad temper, was moody and unpredictable. He needed more help than I could give him. I'd met with his parents several times and begged them to get him professional help, but they refused to accept that there was a problem."

He said nothing and she was grateful, for now that the words were coming, she thought she couldn't stop them if she tried.

"I never crossed the lines of propriety with Bobby. I was his counselor, nothing more." Her voice was more vehement than she intended. "Anyway, one day he went home from school and shot himself." Her throat closed up for a moment, making it difficult for her to breathe.

A frown of sympathy cut across Sawyer's forehead. "I'm sorry."

She gave him a curt nod, fighting tears for the young boy who had died so tragically. "I was so saddened by his death. But I was stunned when a week later the police showed up on my doorstep."

"Why were they there?"

This was the most difficult part to tell, the most difficult part to comprehend. She stared over Sawyer's shoulder, unable to meet his gaze. "It seems Bobby kept a detailed diary on his computer. In the investigation into his death the police had found it and in it Bobby had chronicled a steamy, intimate affair with me."

"But it wasn't true." It was a statement, not a question.

She finally looked at him. "No, it wasn't true. But it was convincing. He'd detailed times and dates, places where we'd had sex. It took almost two weeks for the police to compare my schedule and what I'd really been doing at the times and on the dates Bobby had listed, but by then I'd been tarred and feathered by my friends and coworkers."

"People do love to think the worst," he said softly. She knew he spoke from intimate experience.

"As my coworkers turned away I thought at least I had Scott, the man I'd been dating at the time." She released a small, bitter laugh. "When he asked me if it were true, I knew I didn't want him in my life. The fact that he had to ask made me realize how little he thought of me."

Tears welled up in her eyes, tears for Bobby, for herself. "Anyway, even though I was innocent, I was forced to resign and here I am."

"This explains it." Sawyer got up from his desk and rounded the corner to stand in front of her.

She looked up at him. "Explains what?"

He held out his hand to her and she took it, allowing him to pull her to her feet. He wrapped his arms around her. "Did you think I wouldn't believe you? Did you think that I wouldn't want you to be here with my daughter, with me?"

She squeezed her eyes tightly closed, nodded her head and buried her face in his fresh-scented shirt.

"Amanda, you have nothing to be ashamed of, you did nothing wrong."

"I had to tell you," she said and looked up at him. "You had a right to know. I'll never understand why he wrote those things. He never gave any indication to me that he entertained inappropriate thoughts like that."

"This is why you've believed in me," he whispered in her ear. "Because you know what it's like to be falsely accused, to be looked on with suspicion by people who should know you better."

"That's part of it," she agreed. "But it certainly isn't all of it." For several long moments they remained in each other's arms. She leaned into him, wondering who was drawing strength from whom.

She wanted to weep as she thought of Sawyer in jail. She wanted to take his hand and run with him, far away from Conja Creek and the ordeal he was about to endure.

"Will you be afraid here, just you and Melanie?" he asked.

She considered the question. It had only been twenty-four hours since somebody had crept into the house and hit her over the head.

"No, I won't be afraid," she finally answered. "It's only for a couple of days. You'll be home Monday." She said it with conviction, as if there was no other possibility.

He tightened his arms around her. "I've told Lucas that I want frequent patrols by here while I'm gone."

She finally moved out of his embrace. "We'll be fine. I've spent part of today trying to figure out why I was attacked last night, and I've come to the conclusion that maybe it was an attempted burglary gone bad."

He eyed her with skepticism and she continued. "Think about it, Sawyer. Nothing else makes sense. I haven't made any enemies while I've been here. Nobody will ever make me believe that there's a crazed killer running amok in Conja Creek. Besides, if the person had really wanted to kill me last night I would have been stabbed or shot instead of hit on the head."

His eyes darkened. "I agree with you about that, but I don't want you taking any chances while I'm gone. I want you to be safe."

"We will be," she assured him. "You need to think about yourself now. I'll take care of Melanie and you take care of business so you can come home as soon as possible."

"I'll tell you, right now I'm feeling like the most selfish man on earth."

She looked at him in surprise. "Why?"

"Because I'm about to ask you something that I have no right to ask. I want you in my arms tonight, Amanda. I'm a man with no future, no promises to give, but what I want more than anything on my last night at home is you in my bed. Will you sleep in my bed? In my arms tonight?"

He couldn't want that any more than she did. She

stepped closer to him, her heart beating so hard, so fast she was certain he could hear it. "I want that, too."

As he took her in his arms and kissed her, Helen's words came back to her mind. *I feel evil closing in around us all, an evil that nothing can stop.* Despite the heat of Sawyer's kiss, a cold chill walked up Amanda's spine.

SAWYER STOOD at his bedroom window and watched the sun slowly begin to rise. In the bed behind him Amanda slept, the sound of her slow, easy breathing at odds with the fast pounding of his heart.

In an hour Jackson would arrive to pick him up and take him to jail. Sawyer had arranged for his transfer at the crack of dawn because he hoped to leave the house without any more goodbyes.

After he and Amanda had made love, he'd found it impossible to sleep. He'd spent the long hours of the night going over all the details of Erica's death and the list of potential suspects.

What had been missed?

What clue had been overlooked?

Perfect murders rarely happened, and certainly—contrary to Melanie's claim—no monster had crawled out of the depths of the swamp to brutally stab Erica to death. Whoever had killed Erica had been a monster, but not the kind of childish nightmares.

He turned away from the window and looked at Amanda, his heartbeat slowing a bit as he took in her pretty, slumbering features. She'd been a gift to help him through the last couple of weeks of dark days and nights.

She was the most giving woman he'd ever known. He'd never be able to thank her for her comfort, her courage and support.

She stirred him with her gentle soul and stunned him with the depths of her passion. Making love to Erica had always felt as if he was participating in a sports event. Making love to Amanda felt like coming home.

He'd done everything he could in the short time he'd had to ensure their safety while he was gone. He'd checked and rechecked the security system to make sure everything was functioning properly. He'd also given Amanda his gun, surprised when she'd told him she knew how to use it.

"That's one thing Johnny taught me how to do," she'd told him. "He'd take me out to a shooting range several times a month for practice." There had been a steely resolve in her blue eyes, a resolve that had eased some of his concern. She knew how to use the gun and would do so to save herself, to save his daughter.

Forcing his gaze away from her, he grabbed the stack of clean clothes he'd laid out the night before and carried them out of the bedroom. He would shower and dress in the downstairs bathroom so he wouldn't wake anyone.

He paused outside of Melanie's bedroom, wondering how much a heart, his heart, could hurt before it was irrevocably broken? The realization that he would walk out the front door and not know when he might see her again nearly broke him in two. He finally hurried past her door as he realized he couldn't handle one last look, one last whiff of her sweet, little-girl fragrance.

At least she was talking again. At least he'd have the sound of her whispered, "I love you, Daddy," to take with him this morning.

At precisely six-thirty Sawyer stood at the front door and watched as Jackson's bright red sports car roared up the driveway. Setting the alarm system, then pulling the door closed behind him, Sawyer wondered if he'd ever walk through his front door again.

"I'm not sure the retainer you gave me is big enough to get me up and out this early in the morning," Jackson said as Sawyer opened the passenger door and slid in.

"That retainer was so big you should not only be up early for me but you should also be singing and performing a soft shoe to entertain me."

Jackson grinned. "You really want me to sing, I will, but I remember a time long ago when I was singing in the shower and you told me if I didn't quit the caterwauling you were going to make a kite out of my vocal chords."

Sawyer smiled at the memory. "As I recall, that was the early morning after a late-night keg party."

"Those were the good old days," Jackson said as

he pulled out on the road that would carry them into Conja Creek proper.

"The best," Sawyer agreed.

"There will be more good days, Sawyer," Jackson said. "We're going to get this all behind you and let you get on with the rest of your life." He shot Sawyer a cocky grin. "Hell, man, you've hired the best defense attorney in the entire south."

"And the most humble," Sawyer said drily.

Jackson waved one hand dismissively. "Humility is vastly overrated. It's been my experience that jurors like a man with a little self-confidence." He paused a moment, then continued, "I spoke with the DA last night. I don't think he's going to fight us on bail. Of course, he could always decide to play hardball at the last minute."

"I need to be out," Sawyer said, hating the faint whisper of desperation in his voice. "A killer is walking free, and I need to be home to make sure that Melanie and Amanda stay safe."

Jackson was silent for a long moment, then he sighed. "You know, we've been approaching this as if the murder was all about Erica."

Sawyer eyed him in confusion. "She's the one who wound up dead."

"Yeah, but maybe she wound up dead because somebody wanted to hurt you. Maybe we should be looking into who might have a grudge against you, or at least something to gain by setting you up for the fall."

Sawyer stared out at the passing landscape, the dull throb of a headache beginning to pulse at his temples. "I can't think of anyone who would hate me that much. I can't think of anyone who I would consider an enemy. I was up all night working this from different angles and the only thing that makes sense is that somehow Erica enraged or threatened somebody. Maybe it was whoever fathered the baby she was carrying."

He fell silent as Jackson turned down Main Street and the sheriff's office was visible halfway down the block. A nightmare. He was trapped in a nightmare and couldn't wake up.

Jackson parked in front, cut the engine, then turned to look at Sawyer, no hint of humor in his dark gray eyes. "I'm going to do everything I can to get you out of this mess. My investigator is working day and night on this."

"I know you'll do everything you can," Sawyer replied. "But I've got to be honest with you, at this moment in my life there isn't much you can say that will make me feel any better."

"Understood." Jackson unbuckled his seat belt. "You need a few minutes before we go inside?"

Sawyer drew a deep breath, then unbuckled his belt. "No. Let's just get on with it."

Together the two men got out of the car. Before they could reach the door, Lucas stepped out to greet them. As Sawyer saw the pain that darkened Lucas's eyes, the obvious stress that lined his face,

Sawyer realized his arrest was almost as hard on Lucas as it was on himself.

"Lucas," Jackson greeted him. "You know my client's arrest is a travesty of justice."

"Save it for the courtroom, Jackson," Lucas replied gruffly, his gaze not wavering from Sawyer. "I'm sorry, Sawyer. If I had any control over this it wouldn't be going down this way."

"I'm aware of that," Sawyer said. Did Lucas feel so bad because he knew without a doubt that Sawyer was innocent? Did he know that because he was the monster who had murdered Erica?

Sawyer hated himself for suspecting not only a lifetime friend but also a man who had sworn to protect the people and uphold justice. "So, what happens now?" he asked as the three men entered the building.

"You'll be officially arrested, photographed and fingerprinted," Lucas said. "Then you'll be held in a cell here until your arraignment on Monday morning."

"Before you do all that, have you come up with any leads on the intruder who came into my home and hurt Amanda?"

Lucas shook his head. "Nothing yet."

"You make sure you check George's and Helen's alibis." Although Sawyer would be shocked if either of them had anything to do with the attack, he couldn't discount that both of them made Amanda uneasy.

An edge of anger rose up inside him, anger at the circumstances that had brought him to this time and place. He took a step closer to Lucas, and his anger simmered hotter. "Just keep this in mind, Lucas. While you have me locked up behind bars, the real killer is out there walking the streets. There's a young woman and my daughter without the benefit of a male in the house. You and the DA better pray that nothing happens to them. That's all I've got to say."

Lucas nodded. "Sawyer Bennett, I'm placing you under arrest for the murder of Erica Bennett."

As Lucas read him his rights, visions of Melanie flashed through Sawyer's head, quickly followed by mental pictures of Amanda. He consciously willed them away, and without them he was left with only his stark despair and a horrifying sense that the worst was yet to come.

Chapter Thirteen

Amanda knew he was gone before she opened her eyes. There was an emptiness in the silence that surrounded her that let her know Sawyer had left the building.

She rolled over on her side and opened her eyes in time to see the clock change from four minutes after seven to five after. She closed her eyes once again and thought of the night before.

Their lovemaking had been fierce and intense. Afterward they had clung to each other like two storm-tossed sailors who knew that eventually the sharks would arrive.

Telling him about Bobby had been one of the most difficult things she'd ever done, but once the story was out, she'd been relieved by his response. She cried sometimes for Bobby, who had chosen such a tragic exit from this life. And now she had another child to worry about.

She'd told Sawyer she'd think about staying on

to raise Melanie if he was convicted. It was certainly something she didn't want to agree to without giving it a lot of thought. If she did agree, then she was committing the rest of her life to the little girl. She'd be a single parent to a child who would carry a certain amount of emotional baggage from these events in her life.

There were pros and cons to consider, the biggest pro being that she loved Melanie. And she was in love with Sawyer.

Even if he was released tomorrow and the real culprit was placed behind bars, she suspected her love story with Sawyer wouldn't have a happy ending.

She had no idea how he felt about her. He hadn't told her he loved her. He desired her, that much was clear, but desire without love had no hope for a future. She suspected Lillian was right, that she was an easy convenience in his life. She knew he was grateful to her for her support, but gratitude wasn't the same as love, either.

Knowing that all too soon Melanie would be not only awake but hungry, as well, Amanda got out of bed and padded down the hallway to her own room. Once there she showered quickly, then pulled on a pair of jeans and a T-shirt.

As she walked down the staircase to the lower level, no sounds or scents wafted from the kitchen. Although she missed coming down to the kitchen to fresh coffee already prepared, she was grateful that Sawyer had given Helen some time off.

Amanda would rather be alone in the house with Melanie than have somebody inside whom she didn't trust.

Within minutes she had coffee made and was settled in at the kitchen table with a cup. She faced the window where she could look out to the backyard, and sipped her coffee thoughtfully.

What was happening to Sawyer at this moment? What must he be thinking, feeling? Her heart constricted as she thought of his ordeal.

Funny, but she wasn't afraid to be here alone in the house with Melanie. She trusted that the alarm system would indicate if anyone was trying to break in, and she wouldn't hesitate to use Sawyer's gun to stop an intruder from gaining entrance.

It was possible they might never discover who killed Erica. The best they could hope for was that Jackson Burdeaux could create enough reasonable doubt to see Sawyer free of all the charges against him.

She'd only taken a couple of sips of her coffee when the sounds of soft whining coming through the utility room reminded her that there was a third warm body in the house. Buddy.

The puppy greeted her with a yip of excitement as she opened his crate door. He wiggled himself right into her arms, his little pink tongue licking every place it came into contact with.

As she carried him to the back door she realized that Sawyer probably hadn't considered all the in and out of the house a new dog would require. She grabbed the leash that hung on a hook by the back door and hooked it to Buddy's collar.

"I know training a new puppy isn't in your job description," he'd said to her. Falling in love with him hadn't been in her job description, either.

She peered outside the door and saw nobody around. "Be a good boy and do your business quickly," she said as she punched off the alarm, opened the door, then set him down on the grass next to the back door. He danced around her feet, growled at the leash, then whimpered for her to pick him up. "Come on, Buddy, go potty," she said. He sat and looked up at her, his head cocked to one side. She bent and stood him on his feet. "Come on, Buddy, you can do it." He complied with her wishes, finally squatting and gazing at her with adorable brown eyes.

"Good boy," she exclaimed. "Buddy is a good boy." He bounced back to her arms and she went back into the house, locked the door and reset the alarm. She fed him, then shut him in the utility room and returned to the table.

The sound of footsteps racing down the stairs let her know Melanie had awakened. She came into the kitchen, pink pajamas wrinkled and her long dark hair a cloud of tangles down her back.

"Good morning," Amanda said with forced brightness.

"Morning." Melanie looked around the kitchen in obvious confusion. "Where's Helen?"

"Your daddy gave Helen some time off, so it's just going to be me and you for the next couple of days."

Melanie slid onto the chair opposite her at the table and eyed her dubiously. "Do you know how to cook?"

Amanda smiled. "Probably not as well as Helen, but well enough so we won't starve. In fact, I was just thinking about making some scrambled eggs and toast."

"I like scrambled eggs," Melanie replied. "And sometimes Helen would let me help her cook."

"I was hoping you'd offer to help. I think we'll make a terrific team."

Melanie smiled brightly. "Then let's make some eggs, but first I have to visit Buddy. I'm sure he missed me during the night."

Breakfast preparations were accompanied by Melanie's chatter. It was as if now that she'd found her voice she didn't want a minute to go by without using it.

Amanda didn't mind a bit, but rather savored every word that came out of Melanie's mouth. "I can't wait until Buddy is old enough and smart enough to sleep in my room," she said as they were eating. "Did you have a dog when you were a little girl?"

"No, I didn't."

Melanie frowned sympathetically. "Your mommy wouldn't let you have one?"

"Actually, my mommy and daddy died when I was a little girl and so my aunt and uncle raised me and they didn't like dogs," Amanda said.

Melanie's eyes widened and her lower lip trembled. "Did a swamp monster kill your mommy and daddy?"

"Oh, no, honey. They died in an accident. There was no swamp monster."

Melanie set her fork down next to her plate, her eyes still widened with a touch of fear. "Mommy used to tell me that swamp monsters ate bad little girls, so I try to be a good girl. I really, really try."

"Oh, sweetie, come here." Amanda scooted her chair back from the table and opened her arms to Melanie.

She crawled up on Amanda's lap and wrapped her arms around Amanda's neck. Amanda closed her eyes and held tight, wondering what kind of woman, what kind of mother, would fill her child's head with such nonsense. Still, she knew better than to dismiss the existence of swamp monsters to a child who was certain she'd seen one twice.

"Melanie, honey, your daddy and I would never, ever allow a swamp monster to hurt you." Amanda rubbed her hand down Melanie's slender back. "Even if you were misbehaving, I'd protect you. I'd poke that ugly old swamp monster in his eyes and twist his nose until it looked like a pretzel." Melanie's giggle encouraged Amanda to continue. "I'd bop him over the head with a skillet."

"And pull all his feathers out of his head?" Melanie reared back to look at Amanda.

"Did the swamp monster have feathers on his

head?" she asked. Melanie nodded somberly. "Then I'd pull out every one of those feathers and make a swamp monster pillow out of them that you could punch anytime you wanted to."

Melanie drew in a deep, tremulous breath. "I love you, Amanda." She leaned forward, back into the embrace of Amanda's arms.

"I love you, too," Amanda replied and it was at that moment she knew that if the worst happened and Sawyer was sent away, she could remain here and raise Melanie. She could easily give up her personal life to see that Melanie was loved and felt safe. She had a crazy feeling that fate had arranged everything so she could be here to love this child.

It was just after noon when the phone rang. It was Lillian. "Are we on for lunch and a little shopping spree tomorrow?"

"Can't. Sawyer won't be home so I'm on duty throughout the weekend."

"Is Sawyer working some big project or something?" Lillian asked curiously.

Amanda glanced into the utility room where Melanie was seated on the floor playing with Buddy. She walked to the opposite side of the kitchen before answering, not wanting Melanie to hear what she said. "Sawyer was arrested this morning for Erica's murder."

Lillian gasped. "Oh, no! Is there anything James and I can do? Are you and Melanie all right?"

"Melanie doesn't know what's going on. She

thinks he's on a business trip. We're hoping he'll get bail and be able to come home Monday."

"Oh, hon, you must be so upset. Have Helen make you some of her chocolate delight brownies. You know chocolate really does make you feel better when you're upset."

"Helen is taking some time off so I'm chief cook and bottle washer around here at the moment," Amanda said.

"Get out of town." Lillian sounded more horrified by the idea of no cook in the house than by Sawyer's arrest. "I absolutely insist that you and Melanie come here for dinner tonight. Cook is doing Italian and I know Melanie loves his meatballs and cheese bread."

The invitation wasn't without appeal. If left on their own they were probably looking at a meal of soup and sandwiches. What appealed more than the promise of a good Italian meal was the emotional support she knew Lillian and James would offer.

"And I'll make sure Cook makes something sinfully sweet and chocolate for dessert," Lillian added to sweeten the pot.

"All right," Amanda agreed. Why not? What could it hurt? She and Melanie couldn't be prisoners inside the house. "What time do you want us there?"

"Shall we say sevenish? We'll eat and then I'll take you on a grand tour of the house and my studio."

"Okay, then we'll see you at seven." Amanda carried the cordless phone back to the cradle, then moved to the utility room door. "What do you think about having dinner tonight at James and Lillian's house?" She watched Melanie as she placed Buddy back in the crate.

"Okay," Melanie agreed easily.

"Lillian said it's Italian night."

"Yum-yum. Can we watch a movie on the DVD in the living room?" Melanie asked.

"Sure, sounds like a great way to pass the afternoon." Within minutes the two were seated on the sofa watching one of Melanie's favorite Disney movies.

As Melanie laughed at the antics of the animated creatures, Amanda reached up and touched the back of her head. The wound she'd received when she'd been hit was tender to the touch but seemed to be healing nicely. The injury hurt less than the unanswered questions it had caused. Why me? Why had somebody wanted to hurt her?

She hadn't met many people since arriving in Conja Creek and certainly hadn't had any trouble with anyone. The only thing that made any kind of crazy sense was that she'd been attacked by Helen, and the motive was that Helen was determined to be the only woman in Melanie's life.

Helen fawned over Melanie, encouraged the little girl to spend as much time as possible with her. Wasn't it possible that her love for Melanie had somehow transformed into an obsession—a deadly obsession?

The movie was almost over when the phone rang

again. It was Sawyer, and her heart squeezed into itself at the sound of his familiar but tired voice.

"Lucas let me use the phone," he said. "I wanted to check in and see how you were doing."

"We're doing fine. What about you?" She wanted to reach through the phone line and yank him through, back where he belonged.

"I'm in a cell by myself and they're treating me fine."

"Melanie and I are watching a movie now, then this evening we've been invited to James and Lillian's house for dinner," she said. He replied with a weighty silence. "Sawyer, we can't be prisoners in the house," she added softly.

"I know." He released a heavy sigh. "I just worry."

"And I'll be careful. Besides, I still wonder if Helen isn't behind everything." She kept her voice soft so Melanie wouldn't hear what she said.

"Lucas is checking alibis for the night you were attacked and rechecking hers for the night of Erica's death. At least Helen can't get through the security system. She doesn't know the code. You know to be wary if she shows up at the house for any reason."

"We'll be fine," she assured him once again. "You just focus on what you need to do to get back home to us."

Again there was a weighty pause. "Kiss my daughter for me?"

Tears burned in her eyes as she heard the thick

emotion in his voice. "Tonight and every night until you're home with her again."

"Amanda, whenever you leave the house for anything take my gun with you. I have a sick feeling in my soul that the killer isn't finished yet."

If his wish was to further frighten her with his words, he succeeded. A moment later as she hung up the phone she fought against a terrible sense of foreboding and wondered if she was already marked as the "swamp monster's" next victim?

LUCAS LED SAWYER BACK to his cell after Sawyer finished with his phone call. "Everything all right at home?" Lucas asked.

"As right as it can be under the circumstances," Sawyer replied. He stepped into the cell and winced as the door clanked shut behind him. "Amanda thinks Helen may be responsible for Erica's murder and the attack on Amanda."

Lucas leaned against the wall just beyond the cell bars and shoved his hands into his pockets. "I'll tell you this much, her alibis for both nights are weak. She claims she was in bed asleep on both nights, but since she lives alone there's no way to corroborate the alibis."

Sawyer frowned thoughtfully. "She never tried to hide her feelings about Erica. She hated her. But even given that, I still find it difficult to imagine Helen as a cold-blooded killer."

"Maybe Jackson can use her to create reasonable

doubt for you," Lucas replied. "And in the meantime I'm doing everything possible to solve this case."

"So, you really don't think I'm guilty?" Sawyer realized it mattered to him that Lucas truly believed in his innocence.

"Never did. Still don't." Lucas eyed him curiously. "You still think I slept with your wife?"

Sawyer looked into the eyes of the man he considered one of his closest friends. He'd known Lucas since grade school. Over the years they had shared triumphs and tragedies. "No. I don't believe you slept with her," he finally answered. Nor did he believe that Lucas had anything to do with her death.

Sawyer had been grasping at straws, pointing fingers at somebody, anybody who could be responsible. But he knew in his heart the guilty person wasn't Lucas Jamison.

Sawyer said, "Remember the night in college that I told you I had a bad feeling about you flying home the next day?" Sawyer sat on the lower bunk.

"You screwed around with my alarm clock, and I was nearly two hours late to the airport," Lucas replied.

"But in those two hours your dad's plane mechanic found a problem that in all probability would have resulted in a midair crisis."

"Why are you reminding me of that now?" Lucas asked curiously.

A knot of tension pulsed in Sawyer's jaw. "Because I have that same kind of bad feeling right now." He didn't wait for Lucas to reply, but rather stretched out on the bunk and closed his eyes, hoping, praying that his bad feeling was nothing more than his imagination.

Chapter Fourteen

Amanda pulled away from the house with all her senses on full alert. Melanie was buckled into the passenger seat and thankfully appeared unaware of Amanda's tension.

There's no reason to be nervous, Amanda told herself firmly. She hadn't seen anyone lurking around the house or on the property as she and Melanie had left and gotten into her car. They were only driving a short distance down the road to the Cordells' and she had a loaded gun in her purse as an added measure of security.

The alarm was set on the house, and the doors were locked. She'd left lights on in nearly every room, so they wouldn't return to darkness.

"How do you spend your time when you stay the night with James and Lillian?" Amanda asked as she checked the rearview mirror for the hundredth time. Nobody behind her, nobody in front of her. She liked it that way just fine.

"Sometimes Aunt Lillian and I play dress up. She lets me wear her jewelry and we put on makeup. If she's working in her studio then Uncle James plays games and watches movies with me." Melanie shot her a quick grin. "I always beat him at checkers. I think he lets me win. He told me one time that if he had a little girl he'd want her to be just like me."

"That's nice. So you like spending time with them?" Amanda turned into the Cordells' driveway.

"Not as much as I like spending time with you," Melanie replied. "I wish you could be my mommy."

Amanda's heart stuttered. She pulled up next to Lillian's car, cut the engine, then turned to face Melanie. "Honey, I love you with all my heart, but I can't be your mommy because I'm your nanny."

Melanie's brown eyes darkened. "Well, I'm going to pretend that you're both," she exclaimed firmly as she unbuckled her seat belt.

Amanda was at a loss for words. At that moment the front door of the house opened and Lillian stepped out on the porch. She waved to them, a smile lighting her pretty features. Melanie flew out of the passenger door. "Aunt Lillian, I got a puppy."

"A puppy? And what's your puppy's name?" Lillian asked as Amanda joined them on the porch.

"Buddy, 'cause he's my best buddy after Daddy and Amanda."

"Come inside. Your other buddy, Uncle James, has been waiting for you all afternoon. He's sure that this evening he's finally going to beat you at checkers."

Melanie giggled, then darted into the house ahead of Lillian and Amanda. Lillian shook her head. "What I wouldn't give to have a tenth of her energy." Her smile faded as they stepped into the impressive entryway. She took one of Amanda's hands in hers. "How are you holding up?"

"I'm fine. I'm just hoping the judge sees fit to grant Sawyer bail so he can come back home on Monday." *Please let him come home,* she inwardly prayed.

"Let's all hope that's what happens," Lillian said. "And now come inside and let me show you around. Dinner should be ready in about twenty minutes. I hope you're hungry because I think Cook has outdone himself."

The Cordells' two-story home couldn't have been decorated more differently from Sawyer's. Where Sawyer's was muted colors and sturdy, traditional furnishings, Lillian's dramatic and artistic flair was evident in the living room of her home.

Huge abstract paintings on the walls drew attention with their vivid reds and yellows and splashes of royal blue. The bland, light gray sofa and love seat didn't even attempt to compete with the other items in the room.

A bookcase held exotic-colored vases in unusual shapes and styles. The overall appearance of the room should have radiated chaos, but somehow Lillian had made it all work together to be stunning.

"It's lovely," Amanda said as she walked around, looking at each and every piece.

"Thanks." Lillian grinned. "James is always complaining that the room is overstimulated with color and textures, that he'd prefer something a little more soothing. I always tell him he can have soothing with his next wife."

Amanda laughed. "Like that would ever happen," she replied. "That man is absolutely crazy about you."

Lillian smiled with a touch of smugness. "Please don't let him know that I'm just as crazy about him."

They finished the tour of the house and headed back down the stairs toward the living room. "After we eat I'll take you out to my studio in the back. That's where my heart and soul is."

Dinner was delicious and the conversation pleasant, and for the first time in a week some of Amanda's tension ebbed away. "Guess what I got this afternoon?" James asked Melanie.

"What?" She swiped her mouth with her napkin, erasing the sauce that had decorated her lower lip.

He named the latest popular movie that everyone had been talking about, a new animated film for kids. "I thought maybe after dinner we could pop it in and watch it."

Melanie's eyes brightened with eagerness as she looked at Amanda. "Could we? Could we stay to watch the movie? It would be such fun."

"While they're watching the movie, you and I can go out to the studio," Lillian said. "I've got a coffeemaker out there and a killer caramel coffee to die for."

Amanda hesitated. If they stayed to watch the movie it would be late before they returned home. But as she glanced out the window she realized evening had fallen and night would be here before they left in any case. "Okay," she agreed, deciding an extra hour and a half wouldn't hurt anything.

The rest of the meal passed with conversation about movies and favorite foods and Melanie's new dog. With each moment Amanda found herself relaxing more and more.

This was what life was supposed to be like, good food, good friends and easy conversation. How she wished Sawyer were here sharing it with them. She shoved him out of her mind, not wanting to wonder what he was eating for dinner or how he was spending the long night in a jail cell.

After dinner James and Melanie settled into the living room with the movie playing, and Lillian and Amanda left the house by the back door and headed for what appeared to have once been a carriage house.

As they passed an area of thick brush and trees, Lillian pointed to a small path that was just barely visible in the moonlight illumination. "If you follow that path it will take you right to Sawyer's house. That's how Erica and I used to run back and forth."

When she opened the door to her studio, the scent of turpentine and oil paint drifted out to mingle with the hot night air. "Erica knew that I often worked nights here, so whenever she couldn't sleep or just felt like talking, she'd walk over here and we'd have coffee or she'd call me and we'd meet at her place."

The studio was huge. Along one wall Mardi Gras masks were displayed on hooks. They were stunning, with bright colors and feathers, sequins and rhinestones. "Oh, my gosh," Amanda exclaimed and stepped closer to get a better view of the intricate work involved on each one. "These are absolutely amazing."

"That's my bread and butter. It was never my intention to be known as a mask artist, but I made a couple and they sold and word quickly spread." She gestured Amanda toward a seating area with two chairs, an Oriental rug and a reading lamp. "Sit and I'll make us that coffee."

Amanda sank into one of the chairs as Lillian busied herself at a nearby counter with a sink. "So, if you didn't want to be a mask artist, what kind did you want to be?"

"World renowned." Lillian flashed her a quick smile. "I thought I was going to set the world on fire with my oil paintings. Unfortunately, I suspect the few I've sold have been pity buys from friends."

"I doubt that." Amanda leaned back in the overstuffed chair and gazed at the paintings that hung around the room. "I love the bright colors."

"I have a collection of paintings stored upstairs that are from my dark period," Lillian replied. The scent of rich coffee and sweet caramel filled the air.

"Those are all in shades of blacks and grays and evoke utter despair."

"I can't imagine you creating anything like that," Amanda exclaimed. "You're always so upbeat and full of fun."

Something dark flashed in Lillian's eyes. It was there only a moment, then gone, and she laughed. "My dark period was just a silly phase." She poured the freshly brewed coffee into two oversize earthen mugs. She handed one of them to Amanda, then sat in the chair next to her and breathed a sigh of contentment.

"This is my own little sanctuary. I spend a lot of time working out here, but I also spend a lot of time just being alone. I'm one of those people who require a lot of time alone. Even James knows not to bother me when I'm out here." She paused and took a sip of her coffee and eyed Amanda over the rim of the cup. "I'm surprised you're still here," she said as she lowered the cup from her mouth.

Amanda looked at her blankly. "What do you mean?" she asked in confusion.

"I mean here in Conja Creek. You've been brutally attacked and the man you work for has been arrested for murder. If I were you I'd run, not walk back to Kansas City and put all this behind me."

Amanda took a sip of the sweet coffee, then smiled. "I can't leave now. Aside from the fact that I've allowed my heart to get totally involved with both Sawyer and Melanie, they need me more now than ever."

"But what if Sawyer is convicted? Surely other arrangements will have to be made for Melanie." Lillian reached up and twirled one of her blond curls between two fingers.

"Actually, Sawyer has asked me to stay on in the house and raise Melanie if that happens."

"Really?" Lillian dropped her hand from her hair and looked positively stunned. "You must have made some impression on him. Are you going to do it?"

Amanda sighed. "I don't know. I haven't had much time to process things. On the way over here Melanie told me she wanted me to be her mommy. There's a part of me that would like nothing better."

"How about some cookies to go with the coffee?" Lillian stood abruptly, and her coffee sloshed over the rim of her cup and splashed on the Oriental rug. "How clumsy of me," she exclaimed. She set the cup on the counter, then grabbed a white hand towel.

A slow-building horror filled Amanda as she saw the familiar monogram that decorated the towel— WWW, exactly like the one they'd found in Erica's souvenir box.

SAWYER SAT UP on the bunk as if electrified by the thin mattress beneath him. Since Amanda had found the box of things that had belonged to Erica, the picture frame had tantalized him. And now he remembered where he had seen it before.

That particular frame had held a wedding photo of Lillian and James and had always been displayed on an end table in their living room.

James.

Sawyer had never considered the man a possible suspect, because James had been married to Erica's best friend. Sawyer had been a fool to overlook the obvious, that Erica would have taken deliciously perverse pleasure in seducing her best friend's husband.

Rising from the bunk, Sawyer's mind raced. It certainly would have been convenient for James and Erica to carry on an affair. A short walk through the woods would have put them in each other's arms.

Had James fathered the baby Erica had carried? Had Erica threatened to tell Lillian about the affair, about the baby? Was James the swamp monster Melanie had seen from her bedroom window that night?

James could have easily been watching the house the night that Sawyer had left to go for a walk. He could have then slipped inside to attack Amanda.

Although Sawyer had no idea what motive James might have had to hurt Amanda, it didn't matter. What mattered was that Melanie and Amanda were with James and Lillian tonight and James knew Sawyer was in jail and would be unable to protect the two women he loved.

"Lucas!" The name billowed out of Sawyer on a cloud of fear.

Deputy Maylor stepped through the door. "Sheriff Jamison isn't here. He and everyone but me in the office went to take care of a six-car pileup just north of town."

"You get him on the radio. Tell him it's an emergency. I need to talk to him now." Sawyer grabbed two of the bars that held him captive as a horrible sense of danger welled up inside him.

Chapter Fifteen

"WWW, those are odd initials for you." Amanda was grateful her voice betrayed none of her shock. She'd recognize that towel anywhere.

"James got me these towels last year for Christmas. He told me the initials stand for wild, wonderful woman, but I have a feeling he picked them up cheap on a clearance table in some store." She laughed and threw the towel next to the sink.

James.

Hadn't Lillian told Amanda that Erica had slept with somebody right here in her studio while Lillian had gone to the store?

James.

His name thundered in her head. He'd had an affair with Erica. Amanda knew the certainty of it in her heart, in her soul. And how easily it would have been for him to sneak through the woods that terrible night and confront Erica on the dock.

"You sure you don't want a cookie to go with the

coffee?" Lillian turned and opened one of the cabinet drawers.

"No…thanks." Amanda looked at the display on the wall. A swamp monster, that's what Melanie had said she'd seen, a swamp monster with feathers.

The masks whirled before Amanda's eyes, their creaturelike shapes and feathered heads spinning so fast she felt ill. That's what Melanie had seen—one of Lillian's masks.

The swamp monster smells bad. Melanie's words thundered through Amanda's head. Turpentine, was that what swamp monsters smelled like? Turpentine and oil paint? How could they have been so blind? Why hadn't they realized it was James?

"Actually, I'm not feeling very well." Amanda was sickened by her suspicions. They hadn't considered him a viable suspect before because of the strength of his marriage to Lillian, because of his apparent commitment to his wife. But now she wondered how much of that had been nothing more than a facade, a pretense to hide an affair with the neighbor next door.

Did Lillian know? Did she even suspect her husband's infidelity or her best friend's utter betrayal?

"I think I'll just get Melanie and we'll head on home. She can watch the movie another time." Amanda stood.

"I'm afraid I can't let you do that," Lillian said, and turned from the cabinet to face Amanda.

Amanda stared at her blankly, trying to make sense of the gun Lillian pointed at her chest.

"Amanda, Amanda." Lillian shook her head sadly. "I warned you not to get too close to Sawyer. After I hit you over the head that night I'd hoped you'd be frightened enough to go back where you came from. But you are stubborn, if nothing else."

Shock waves crashed through Amanda as she grappled to make sense of things. "You attacked me? But why?" Body tensed with fight-or-flight adrenaline, Amanda wanted, needed answers. She somehow needed to know what on earth was going on.

"Because you're screwing things up." Lillian's voice rose, and for an instant her eyes shone with a crazed fever.

"Lillian, put the gun down and let's talk." Amanda tried to keep her voice as soft and on as even a keel as possible. "I'm sure this is all just a misunderstanding. Put down the gun and we'll talk."

"No misunderstanding," she replied. "You're in my way, and now I have to get rid of you."

Amanda felt as if she'd slipped into an alternate universe. Although on some primal level she knew she was in danger, she still hoped to figure out exactly why this was happening. She still hoped she could talk her way out of this.

"Lillian, I thought we were friends. Can't we talk this out without the gun?"

"We are friends," she replied. "But sometimes friendship isn't enough." She motioned with the gun toward the studio door. "We're going to take a walk."

Amanda knew if they left the studio the level of

danger would increase. She didn't know what was going through Lillian's head, but it was obvious the woman wasn't rational.

"Lillian, please. Tell me what's wrong," she stalled.

"There's nothing wrong now. After you're gone everything will fall into place. None of this would have happened if Erica had been reasonable, but she was such a selfish, hateful woman."

All the blood in Amanda's body froze. "You?" The word whispered out of her. "You killed Erica? Was it because she had an affair with James?"

Lillian's features transformed into something hard and ugly. "I should have killed her for that… James, too. That night, the night of the murder, James came to me and confessed everything. He'd been weak and Erica had been persuasive. They'd been carrying on for two months. He was through with her, promised me he'd never see her again, and then he told me Erica was pregnant with his child."

She stepped closer to Amanda, the gun never wavering from its target. "After James confessed, I came out here and sat and thought about things and I realized all of it might be a blessing in disguise. She was carrying James's baby, the baby I'd never been able to give him. God, but I'd wanted a baby so badly, but I couldn't have one. That's why I had my dark period."

She frowned for a moment, the gesture tugging her pretty features into something nearly unrecognizable. "I called Erica that night and told her to meet me on the dock. I told her I'd made a new mask and wanted to show it off to her."

As Lillian spoke, Amanda tried to absorb what she was saying and at the same time tried to find something, anything that might be used as a weapon. But there was nothing to compete with the gun Lillian held.

"I grabbed a mask and went to the dock," Lillian continued. "Erica was there waiting for me. She had the knife with her. She told me she was going to carve the initials of all her lovers into the dock. I asked her if James's initials would be one of the first or one of the last she carved."

Amanda dismissed the idea of screaming for help. Who would rush to save her? James? He had to know that his wife was responsible for Erica's murder and had done nothing about it. Besides, the last thing Amanda wanted to do was draw Melanie's attention. She had no idea how much trauma the child could endure before she fractured apart forever.

"She told me not to look so serious, that she was just passing time with James until somebody better, more exciting came along. I didn't go there to kill her," Lillian said. "I told her I didn't care about the affair. All I cared about was the baby…James's baby. I wanted her to have the baby and give it to us. Then James and I would have the family we always wanted and Erica could go on her merry way."

Lillian's voice grew more shrill with each word

and the hand holding the gun trembled violently. Amanda didn't move a muscle, afraid that the blink of an eye, a jerk of her head might cause Lillian's finger to twitch on the trigger.

"She laughed at me." Hysteria forced Lillian's voice up an octave. "She told me she was going to have an abortion, that there was no way she was going to go through another pregnancy. She wasn't going to get fat and hormonal for anybody. I got so angry and suddenly we were fighting and the knife was in my hand and I stabbed her and stabbed her and—"

She drew a deep breath as if to steady herself. "Melanie must have seen the mask on the dock and in her confusion didn't realize it was me. The movie is going to be over soon and the last thing I want to do is upset Melanie, so you and I are going to take a walk. And if you don't do what I say I'll shoot you right here and let Melanie see your blood splattered all over the walls. Now move slow and easy and get outside."

"But I still don't understand," Amanda said as she walked to the door. "Why are you doing this to me?"

"I told you why," Lillian replied as the two of them stepped out into the hot, humid night air. "Because you're in the way."

"In the way of what?" Amanda blinked against the sting of hot tears.

"I had it all worked out. Sawyer goes to prison for Erica's murder, and James and I raise Melanie. We're her godparents, you know. But then you came along and screwed it all up." The hardness was back in Lillian's eyes, a killing hardness that expanded the knot of terror in Amanda's chest. "Walk, Amanda. I'm tired of talking." Lillian pointed to the dark path that led to Sawyer's property.

Help me, a voice inside Amanda screamed. *Dear God, help me.* Her thoughts raced a frenzied path through her head. She couldn't outrun a bullet. It also didn't appear as if she was going to be able to talk her way out of this.

Nobody but Sawyer knew where she was, and he was locked up behind bars and would never know what had happened.

"You'll never get away with this, Lillian," she said as the woods closed in around them. "You won't be able to blame my death on Sawyer." She stopped walking, then gasped as the barrel of the gun jabbed her in the back.

"Keep walking." Lillian's voice held the cool command of determination.

Under ordinary circumstances, anyone would probably be afraid to be in the woods in the dark, but the night and the nearby swamp held no terror to compare to that of Lillian's gun pressed painfully against Amanda.

"Where are we going?" she asked as her gaze went first to the left, then to the right, seeking an escape route.

"To the dock. We're going to have a fight. When you're dead, I'll call the police and tell them you attacked me, that we were arguing because I wondered out loud about Sawyer's innocence. You went crazy and pulled a gun. We wrestled and the gun went off, tragically killing you."

This woman might win. She might not only kill Amanda but also gain custody of Melanie. The very idea of Lillian raising the little girl Amanda had grown to love created a soul-stirring white heat of rage in Amanda.

She would not be a prop in Lillian's drama, and she refused to walk dutifully to her death. If she could somehow escape Lillian and make it to Sawyer's house she could throw something through the window and set off the alarm, and the alarm would summon help.

Escape. The word thundered in her head to the beat of her frantic heart. She hadn't been able to save Bobby, but she'd do whatever possible to see that Lillian didn't achieve her ultimate goal. Amanda had to stay alive to save Melanie.

Each step took them deeper into the woods. Insects whirred and buzzed an incessant tune. The scent of decaying vegetation and fish grew more pronounced, telling Amanda they were precariously close to the swamp water.

The moonlight disappeared, unable to break through the snarled tangle of branches overhead. Beneath their feet thick vines crossed the path, making the footing treacherous.

"I'll be a good mother, you'll see," Lillian muttered beneath her breath. "I should have had a baby of my own. I wanted one more than anything in the world, but now it's okay. Now I'll have Melanie. We'll be the family we should have been."

She's crazy, Amanda thought. Crazy and ruthless, a deadly combination. She'd already killed once, and there would be no hesitation in killing again.

Amanda knew if she was going to make a move it had to be now, here where the darkness was almost impenetrable.

Amanda's heart rate reached a fever pitch. There were only two outcomes to what she was about to do. She'd either survive or she wouldn't.

With a silent prayer, she threw herself to the ground and rolled off the path.

SAWYER PACED the cell like an agitated lion. He told himself that his anxiety level was way out of proportion, that even if James had killed Erica that didn't mean that Melanie and Amanda were now in imminent danger.

He summoned to his head words of comfort, of calm rational thinking, but all of it was chased away by the irrational gut-wrenching feeling of something bad happening just out of his reach.

"Maylor!" He yelled for the young deputy, who seemed to be the only person in the station besides Sawyer. "Did you get Lucas on the radio?" he asked when Maylor appeared in the doorway.

"He's on his way back here now," Maylor replied. "Should be here in the next couple of minutes."

"Tell him I need to talk to him the minute he comes in." Sawyer went back to the bunk and threw himself down, once again seeking some internal assurance that everything was all right.

But by the time Lucas came in, Sawyer was once again pacing the floor, every nerve ending in his body screaming alarm. "You've got to let me out of here," he said to Lucas. "I need to check on Melanie and Amanda."

"You know I can't do that." Lucas looked pained. "I'll check on them. They're at your place, right?"

"They're at the Cordells'. Lucas, I think James killed Erica." He quickly filled Lucas in on what thoughts had been whirling around in his head. "Don't call over there. If what I think is true, then we don't know how desperate he might be. We can't be sure what he's capable of."

Sawyer grabbed the bars so tightly his knuckles turned white. "Let me go over there. For God's sake man, it's my daughter who might need me. I swear if you let me go, I'll come right back here if I see that they're okay."

Lucas hesitated and Sawyer pushed him harder. "You know you can trust me to turn myself back in. I've got that bad feeling in my soul. They need me. Let me go, Lucas. For the Brotherhood."

Reluctantly Lucas pulled his keys from his pocket. "You're going to get my ass fired sure as

I'm standing here." He paused with the key in his hand. "I'll let you out on one condition. You remain in my custody. I'll drive out to the Cordells' and when we get there you remain in the car. No funny business, Sawyer."

"Fine. Just hurry."

Minutes later the two were in Lucas's patrol car heading toward the Cordell house. Deputy Maylor followed behind them in his own car. He would provide backup should they encounter any problems.

It was a silent, tense ride. Sawyer fought against the overriding sense of doom that threatened to swallow him. His palms were damp with anxiety, and his heart raced from the effects of adrenaline.

Amanda's car was parked in the driveway, and the sight of it alleviated some of Sawyer's fear. Surely he'd overreacted. Surely they were all inside, safe and sound, having just finished a pleasant meal. There was no reason for James to go after Melanie or Amanda.

Sawyer watched as Lucas and Ed Maylor went to the front door. James answered, and the two officials disappeared into the house. A moment later Lucas came out alone. Unable to sit another minute, Sawyer got out of the patrol car. "What's going on?"

"James and Melanie are inside. They were watching a movie. He said that Lillian and Amanda are out in the studio."

Knowing that Maylor was inside the house and Melanie was safe, Sawyer's thoughts turned to

Amanda. If James was in the house, then surely she was okay.

Sawyer and Lucas had just rounded the house and were almost at the studio when a crack of gunfire coming from the nearby woods exploded the silence of the night.

AMANDA SWALLOWED the scream that clawed up the back of her throat as the bullet that Lillian had fired slammed into a tree trunk mere inches from her head. Silence followed the shot, the waiting silence of a hunter seeking prey.

Amanda was afraid to move, knowing that the snap of a branch, the rustle of a vine would alert Lillian to her location.

"Come out, come out, wherever you are." Lillian's whisper dripped malevolence. Amanda's heart beat so hard, so fast she wondered if Lillian could hear it. She tried to see where the other woman was, tried to hear anything that would let her know how close Lillian was to her.

The second shot kicked up brush inches in front of where Amanda lay on her side. *Move!* A voice in her head screamed the alarm. *For God's sake move before she finds you!*

Wasn't a moving target more difficult to hit than a static one? Drawing a deep breath, Amanda sprang to her feet and crashed through the underbrush in the direction of Sawyer's house.

Although there was no resulting gunfire, Amanda heard the sound of Lillian's pursuit. Thrashing brush, the pound of footsteps. A sob ripped from Amanda as a tree branch slapped her face and thick kudzu vines threatened to snag her and hold her captive.

To her right the sound of something big splashing in the water let her know another hunter had captured some prey. Amanda's terror flamed hotter.

She had to stay alive for Melanie's sake. She had to escape to tell somebody about Lillian so that Sawyer didn't spend the rest of his life in prison for a murder he hadn't committed.

Lillian's labored breathing seemed to warm the back of Amanda's neck as she fought her way through the darkness, through the woods.

She suspected the only reason Lillian hadn't fired again was because she didn't have a clear shot and didn't want to waste a bullet.

Somewhere in the back of her mind Amanda knew that once she reached the clearing of Sawyer's property she would be most vulnerable. She had only two choices, remain in the woods until Lillian managed to get off a lucky shot or expose herself and pray she could make it to the house and set off the alarm. Neither choice offered much hope.

However, Amanda was an optimist. She had no weapon, no way to defend herself, but she was armed with a healthy dose of hope. The streak of optimism burned brighter inside her as she saw the clearing ahead.

The tall rosebushes in Sawyer's backyard might provide some cover. There were several trees and the patio furniture.

All she really needed to do was make it to the patio, grab a chair and smash the glass of the French doors. The alarm would ring and surely she'd be able to hide from Lillian in the big house until help arrived.

She burst into the clearing, legs pumping and lungs threatening to explode. She refused to look behind but kept her focus on the house in the near distance.

I'm going to make it, she thought. *I can make it!* She pushed harder, running faster than she'd ever run in her life. As she ran she heard the sweet sound of Melanie's laughter ringing in her head, felt the warmth of her little hand in hers.

Those images were replaced with ones of Sawyer, his eyes gleaming with desire as his lips curved into a tender smile. She tasted the fire of his lips as she ignored the stitch in her side.

She was almost to the back porch when the gun cracked again. Instantaneously pain seared through her thigh, and her leg buckled beneath her, throwing her facedown on the ground.

For a moment she was so stunned she couldn't move. The agony in her thigh ripped through her. Through a haze of pain she rolled over on her back to see Lillian standing over her, the gun pointed at Amanda's head.

At that moment Amanda's hope ebbed away,

like the blood that bubbled warm and sticky out of her thigh.

She closed her eyes, not wanting to see death's delivery and instead thought of Sawyer and Melanie and prayed that somehow, someway they would be all right.

"Lillian!" The familiar deep male voice boomed like thunder in the night.

As Lillian turned toward Sawyer's frantic voice, Amanda kicked with both legs, connecting with Lillian's knees. With a scream, Lillian stumbled backward and fell to the ground.

In an instant Lucas had kicked her gun away and had her in custody. Sawyer rushed to Amanda, a sob ripping from his throat as he gathered her into his arms. "Get an ambulance, she's hurt," he yelled at Lucas, then gazed down at her. "It's all right now," he said softly. "Amanda, do you hear me? Everything is going to be just fine."

"Melanie?" she asked.

"She's okay. She's safe."

"Wh-what are you doing here? You're supposed to be in jail."

He smiled, a tense smile that didn't quite touch his eyes. "It's a long story, but I'm here now and we're going to get you help."

"This definitely wasn't in my job description," she said, surprised that her voice sounded very faraway as darkness closed in around her.

Chapter Sixteen

Amanda stood at the window in her bedroom and stared out at the lawn where Buddy and Melanie were playing under Helen's watchful eye. Sawyer was downstairs in his study. He'd decided that Bennett Architectural Enterprises could just as easily be conducted from here as from an office in town. Earlier that morning he'd landed a huge job that would keep him busy for the next couple of months.

It had been ten days since that horrible night when Amanda had nearly lost her life. Lillian had confessed to Erica's murder and to plotting to see Sawyer in prison so she could raise her goddaughter.

Thankfully, the wound on Amanda's thigh had been superficial, and although there would probably be a scar it would be nothing compared to the scar she'd carry in her heart.

James had put the Cordell house up for sale and had left town. The most difficult part of everything was trying to find a rational explanation for Lillian's actions for Melanie. Amanda and Sawyer had finally agreed to tell Melanie that her aunt Lillian had been sick and it had been her sickness that had made her do bad things. Melanie accepted that explanation and they all spoke no more about Lillian.

She turned away from the window and eyed her packed suitcase. It was time to go. She'd awakened that morning and realized she couldn't spend another day here.

In the past ten days, life in the Bennett house had found a comforting normalcy, and Amanda had no place. Melanie had her voice, and Sawyer had his freedom, and there was nothing more Amanda could do except tell them goodbye and get on with her own life.

Sawyer had been attentive and caring since the attack, but there had been nothing between them that had crossed the line of employee and employer.

Melanie, knowing that the swamp monster had been caught and put into jail, was coming out of her shell, eager to spend time with her friends and looking forward to school in the fall.

Staying here would be torture. Amanda had made the mistake of falling in love with Sawyer, and she could no longer be his nanny and occasional convenient bed partner. She needed more. She deserved more.

She had come here seeking some redemption for Bobby's suicide and in many ways she'd found it. She'd realized that she'd done everything she could have possibly done for Bobby, and it wasn't her fault that it wasn't enough. It had been a tragedy... just like Lillian was a tragedy.

She'd been a woman driven by demons Amanda couldn't begin to understand. Erica might have been a shallow thrill seeker but Lillian had been a different monster altogether.

Grabbing her suitcase, she drew a deep breath for what lay ahead. She'd given Sawyer and Melanie no warning that she was leaving today. She'd known that saying goodbye would be more difficult for her than facing death at Lillian's hands in the middle of the dark swamp.

As she walked down the stairs, the sound of Melanie's laughter and Buddy's sharp yips of excitement drifted in through the French doors. She was comforted by the sound. Melanie was going to be just fine. Sawyer was a sensitive, caring father and he would see to it that she was okay.

When she reached the study door, she dropped her suitcase on the floor just outside, then stepped in. Sawyer was seated at his desk and looked up, his lips curving into a smile that shot straight to her heart.

"Hey, you," he said, then frowned. "Are you all right?"

She nodded, swallowing against the thick emotion that suddenly rose up in her throat. "I...I'm leaving."

"Okay, when will you be back?"

"I mean, I'm leaving for good."

He shot out of the chair and came around the

desk to face her, confusion darkening his eyes. "What do you mean leaving for good? What's going on, Amanda?"

She'd known it was going to be hard, but his concern made it even more difficult than she'd imagined. "You don't need me anymore. Melanie doesn't need me. You've got your life back, Sawyer. You're going to be working here during the days, and in the fall Melanie will go back to school."

"But that doesn't mean we don't need you," he protested. He placed his hands on her shoulders, and the familiar touch, the scent of his cologne, forced tears to her eyes.

She blinked them away and stepped back, forcing him to drop his arms to his sides. "I can't stay, Sawyer." She couldn't look at him, but rather stared at the wall just over his left shoulder. "I've made the incredible mistake of falling in love with you." She looked at him then and saw the stricken look on his face.

"Amanda…I…"

She held up a hand to stop whatever he was about to say. "Please, it's my problem, not yours. So much has happened in your life while I've been here. I never expected anything from you but a job, and I don't expect anything now." The tears she had tried so hard to suppress now fell freely down her cheeks. "Just let me go, Sawyer. I need to find my own life now."

His face displayed a dozen emotions but finally settled on one of resignation, an acceptance that broke what was left of her heart. It wasn't until that moment that she realized she'd hoped for something different. Someplace in the back of her ever-optimistic mind, she'd hoped that he'd take her in his arms and tell her he loved her, that he couldn't live without her.

"You going back to Kansas City?" he asked.

She nodded. "I called Johnny this morning and told him I'd be home sometime tomorrow evening. I'll stay with him until I can get an apartment and take my things out of storage."

"Melanie will be upset."

"Only for a short time," she replied. "I'll do my best to make it okay with her. Children are resilient, and besides, she has a wonderful father who will get her through any rough patches." She tried to offer him a smile, but once again felt the press of hot tears. "I'll just go tell her goodbye now."

She fled from the office where they had spent so much time together and headed for the French doors. She nodded to Helen, who sat at the patio table. She and Helen had talked for a long time two days earlier. Amanda had apologized for suspecting Helen, and Helen had graciously accepted the apology.

"Melanie, I need to talk to you," Amanda said. "Can you put Buddy on his leash for a minute and let Helen hang on to him?"

"Okay." It took the little girl only a couple of minutes to get the rambunctious puppy under control and hand the leash to Helen, then she raced to Amanda and looked up at her expectantly.

It was going to be every bit as difficult telling Melanie goodbye as it had been telling Sawyer. Amanda crouched down so she was eye level with Melanie. "Honey, it's time for me to leave."

The smile that had lifted the corners of Melanie's lips disappeared. "Where are you going?"

"I'm going home, back to Kansas City."

Melanie hugged Amanda, her little body warm as she pressed closer. "When will you be back?"

"I don't think I'm coming back."

Melanie's dark brown eyes radiated disbelief. "Yes, you are. You have to come back 'cause I love you. Daddy and I need you here with us." She wrapped her arms around Amanda's neck.

"You and your daddy are going to be just fine without me," Amanda replied as she hugged Melanie tight. "Now you have Buddy, and we both know he's a smart, good dog."

"I love Buddy, but I love you, too," Melanie exclaimed as she tightened her arms around Amanda's neck.

"We can write and e-mail each other every day." Amanda fought against her own tears. "And I'll call you as often as you want."

"I don't want to write or e-mail you. I don't want to talk to you on the phone. I want you here!" Melanie's voice grew thick with tears as Sawyer stepped out onto the patio.

Melanie pulled herself from Amanda's arms and ran directly to her father. "Make her stay, Daddy. Tell her not to go."

Sawyer scooped her up in his arms and hugged her to his chest. "I can't make her stay, Melanie. Amanda has to go on with her life."

Amanda stood, the finality of his words thrumming through her. It was time to go. The more quickly she left, the less painful the goodbye. She said nothing more but left the patio, went back inside and grabbed her suitcase, then walked out the front door.

Within minutes she was in her car driving away from the Bennett house and Conja Creek. The landscape flew by in a mist of tears. She hadn't realized how much she'd begun to think of Sawyer's house as home until now as she left. She hadn't realized just how deeply woven into her heart he and Melanie had been until now as her heart unraveled.

You can get through this, she told herself and tightened her fingers around the steering wheel. She was strong. That night with Lillian in the woods she'd recognized just how strong she could be.

She would rebuild a life in Kansas City. She'd no longer hide in her apartment, afraid of what people might say as they speculated on her relationship with Bobby. She knew she'd done nothing wrong and she would hold her head high.

Eventually maybe she'd find love again, but she knew no man would ever be able to touch her as Sawyer had. She couldn't even be bitter or angry that he hadn't really loved her. She'd simply come along at the wrong time in his life.

She'd been driving for about twenty minutes when she looked in her rearview mirror and saw a police car behind her, the cherry lights on top flashing. A glance at her speedometer made her realize she'd been speeding.

Terrific, she'd not only be leaving Louisiana with a broken heart, but was probably going to carry away a speeding ticket, as well.

She pulled over to the side of the road, watching in her mirror as the police car parked just behind her. She grabbed her purse from the seat next to her and dug into it for her driver's license, then rolled down her window to face the policeman.

"Lucas!" she said in surprise as he appeared at the window.

"I need you to get out of the car, Amanda."

"Get out of the car?" She looked at him in confusion. Why would he need her to get out of the car for a speeding ticket? And wasn't this somewhat out of his jurisdiction?

"Please, out of the car." He didn't offer her a smile.

"I know I was maybe speeding a little. Is something else wrong?" she asked as she opened the door and stepped out. Maybe this was normal procedure in these parts of the country. She held out her driver's license, but he ignored it.

"You want to step back to my car?"

"Lucas, please. What's going on?" she asked as

she walked with him to his car. "Has something happened? Is something wrong?" Panic torched up inside her as she thought of Sawyer and Melanie.

"It's kind of an emergency," Lucas replied, and she noticed there was a definite sparkle in his eyes. He opened the back door and motioned her inside.

Sawyer sat in the backseat. She hesitated a moment, then climbed in next to him. Lucas slammed the door closed and leaned against the car as if he had nothing better to do than park on the side of the highway and watch the grass grow.

"Sawyer, what's going on?" she asked. "Is Melanie okay?"

"She's fine. Forgive the drama, but after you left I realized there were some things I hadn't said to you. I knew I'd have a hard time catching up with you on the road. You had too big a head start, so I went to Lucas and told him it was vital that we catch up with you."

She stared at him, trying to absorb his presence here. "What things did you not say to me?" she asked, her heart beating with an unsteady rhythm.

His green eyes held her gaze intently, then he laughed softly. "You are some piece of work, Amanda Rockport. You flew in at the worst possible time of my life and brought a calm sanity and a steadfast belief in me that I desperately needed."

So, he wanted to thank her? Was that why he was here? Because he'd forgotten to thank her before she'd walked out of his life?

In the close quarters of the backseat of the patrol car, her senses swam with him. His cologne eddied in the air, and the heat from his body evoked memories of being held in his arms.

"If you stopped me because you forgot to say thank-you, then you're welcome," she said stiffly. All she wanted to do was throw herself in his arms, but she refused to humiliate herself that way. She'd already bared her heart to him. There was nothing else for her to say.

"No, that's not why I'm here, although I'll always be grateful to you. But this has nothing to do with gratitude." His eyes darkened slightly. "You shocked me, leaving so quickly without any warning. I hadn't had a chance to sort through my feelings for you. I thought we'd have more time together."

She didn't say anything because she didn't know what to say. He knew how she felt about him, but she still didn't know why he was here.

He reached out and took her hand, and she wondered if he was somehow trying to torture her? But she didn't pull her hand away, couldn't, even if she wanted to. Instead she twined her fingers with his.

"At first I thought my feelings for you were nothing but gratitude. You'd saved my sanity and, more important, you'd put your life on the line to keep Lillian from taking my daughter. Then I thought what I felt for you was nothing more than passion. Making love with you was incredible."

She wanted to scream, to pound his chest and ask

him what he was doing to her? Instead she stared at him with intensity and held her breath.

He smiled. "The minute I watched your car drive down my driveway my feelings all came together and I realized exactly what I felt for you. I'd thought I'd made the worst mistake of my life by marrying Erica. But just after you left I realized if I let you go that would be the biggest mistake of my life."

His words caused her heart to fly, but the flight was short-lived. She pulled her hand from his and searched the face that she loved, those beautiful green eyes and strong, bold features. "This isn't about Melanie, is it? I know she was upset that I was leaving."

"Amanda." His voice held a gentle chide. "I love my daughter with all my heart, but I'm here because I love you and I want to build a life with you. It has absolutely nothing to do with the fact that Melanie adores you. That's just icing on the cake."

She stared at him, wanting to believe what she thought she'd heard him say. "Say it again," she whispered.

"What, that Melanie adores you?" He gazed at her teasingly.

"No, the other part. The part just before that." She wanted to make sure she hadn't imagined it, that she hadn't just heard what she so desperately wanted to hear.

He smiled then, that devastating smile that fired through her heart. "I love you, Amanda. Stay with me, not because we need you, but because I want you in my life forever."

The words were barely out of his mouth and she was half on his lap, claiming his mouth with her own. He wrapped her in his arms and his heart was pounding against her own.

The kiss was deep and filled with all the longing she possessed for him. She tasted not only passion in his lips, but also a sweet commitment she'd always dreamed of.

The kiss finally ended, and he smiled at her. "You know, this isn't exactly in your job description," he teased.

She laughed, joy filling her soul as she thought of the future. "Come on, let's get out of here and into my car."

He nodded. "Yes, it's time to go home."

It was rumored that he'd killed his wife and tried to feed her to the gators, but now everyone knew the truth, and Amanda intended to spend the rest of her life not as a nanny, but as a wife to the man who had stolen her heart.

* * * * *

Melita had been expecting a chaste quick kiss of the generic variety. But this kiss with Sully was the kind that sparked a dying flame to life. The kind of kiss you can't plan for. The kind of kiss memories are built on.

The memory of her murdered lover, Nemo, came to her then and she made a starved little noise in the back of her throat. She raised her arms and threaded her fingers through Sully's hair, pulled him closer. Felt his body settle, then melt into her.

In that instant her hunger for him grew, and his for her. She pressed herself to him with more urgency, and he responded in kind.

Melita came out of her kiss-induced memory of

Nemo with a start. "Wait a minute." She pushed Sully away from her. "You bastard!"

She spit two nasty words at him in Greek, then wiped his kiss from her lips.

"I thought you deserved some solid proof that I'm still in one piece." He started for the door. "The clock's ticking, honey. Come on, let's get out of here."

"That's it? You sucker me into kissing you, and that's all you have to say?"

"I'm sorry. How's that?"

He didn't sound sorry in the least. "You're—"

"Getting out of this godforsaken prison cell. Stop whining and let's go."

"Not if I was being shot at sunrise. Go. You deserve whatever you get if you walk out that door."

He turned back. "Freedom is what I'm going to get."

"A second of freedom before the guards in the hall shoot you." She jammed her hands on her hips. "And to think I was worried about you."

"If you're staying behind, it's no skin off my ass."

"Wait! What about our deal?"

"You just said you're not coming. Make up your mind."

"Have you forgotten we need a boat?"

"How could I? You keep harping on it."

"I'm not going without a boat. And those guards out there aren't going to just let you walk out of here. You need me and we need a plan."

"I already have a plan. I'm getting out of here. That's the plan."

"I should have realized that you never intended to take me with you from the very beginning. You're a liar and a coward."

Of everything she had read, there was nothing in Sully Paxton's file that hinted he was a coward, but it was the one word that seemed to register in that one-track mind of his. The look he nailed her with a second later was pure venom.

He came at her so quickly she didn't have time to get out of his way. "You know I'm not a coward."

"Prove it. Give me until dawn. I need one more night to put everything in place before we leave the island."

"You're asking me to stay in this cell one more night...and trust you?"

"Yes."

He snorted. "Yesterday you knew they were planning to harm me, but instead of doing something about it you went to bed and never gave me a second thought. Suppose tonight you do the same. By tomorrow I might damn well be in my grave."

"Okay, I screwed up. I won't do it again." Melita sucked in a ragged breath. "I can't leave this minute. Dawn, Sully. Wait until dawn." When he looked as if he was about to say no, she pleaded, "Please wait for me."

"You're asking a lot. The door's open now. I

would be a fool to hang around here and trust that you'll be back."

"What you can trust is that I want off this island as badly as you do, and you're my only hope."

"I must be crazy."

"Is that a yes?"

"Dammit!" He turned his back on her. Swore twice more.

"You won't be sorry."

He turned around. "I already am. How about we seal this new deal?"

He was staring at her lips. Suddenly Melita knew what he expected. "We already sealed it."

"One more. You enjoyed it. Admit it."

"I enjoyed it because I was kissing someone else."

He laughed. "That's a good one."

"It's true. It might have been your lips, but it wasn't you I was kissing."

"If that's your excuse for wanting to kiss me, then—"

"I was kissing Nemo."

"What's a nemo?"

Melita gave Sully a look that clearly told him that he was trespassing on sacred ground. She was about to enforce it with a warning when a voice in the hall jerked them both to attention.

She bolted away from the wall. "Get back in bed. Hurry. I'll be here before dawn."

She didn't reach the door before he snagged her

arm, pulled her up against him and planted a kiss on her lips that took her completely by surprise.

When he released her, he said, "If you're confused about who just kissed you, the name's Sully. I'll be here waiting at dawn. Don't be late."

ATHENA FORCE

Heart-pounding romance and thrilling adventure.

History repeats itself...unless she can stop it.

Investigative reporter Winter Archer is thrown into writing
a biography of Athena Academy's founder. But someone
out there will stop at nothing—not even murder—to
ensure that long-buried secrets remain hidden.

ATHENA FORCE

Will the women of Athena unravel Arachne's powerful
web of blackmail and death...or succumb to their
enemies' deadly secrets?

Look for

VENDETTA

by *Meredith Fletcher*

*Available November
wherever you buy books.*

REQUEST YOUR FREE BOOKS!

2 FREE NOVELS PLUS 2 FREE GIFTS!

HARLEQUIN®

INTRIGUE®

Breathtaking Romantic Suspense

YES! Please send me 2 FREE Harlequin Intrigue® novels and my 2 FREE gifts. After receiving them, if I don't wish to receive any more books, I can return the shipping statement marked "cancel." If I don't cancel, I will receive 6 brand-new novels every month and be billed just $4.24 per book in the U.S., or $4.99 per book in Canada, plus 25¢ shipping and handling per book and applicable taxes, if any*. That's a savings of close to 15% off the cover price! I understand that accepting the 2 free books and gifts places me under no obligation to buy anything. I can always return a shipment and cancel at any time. Even if I never buy another book from Harlequin, the two free books and gifts are mine to keep forever.

182 HDN EEZ7 382 HDN EEZK

Name	(PLEASE PRINT)	
Address		Apt. #
City	State/Prov.	Zip/Postal Code

Signature (if under 18, a parent or guardian must sign)

Mail to the **Harlequin Reader Service®**:
IN U.S.A.: P.O. Box 1867, Buffalo, NY 14240-1867
IN CANADA: P.O. Box 609, Fort Erie, Ontario L2A 5X3

Not valid to current Harlequin Intrigue subscribers.

Want to try two free books from another line?
Call 1-800-873-8635 or visit www.morefreebooks.com.

* Terms and prices subject to change without notice. NY residents add applicable sales tax. Canadian residents will be charged applicable provincial taxes and GST. This offer is limited to one order per household. All orders subject to approval. Credit or debit balances in a customer's account(s) may be offset by any other outstanding balance owed by or to the customer. Please allow 4 to 6 weeks for delivery.

Your Privacy: Harlequin is committed to protecting your privacy. Our Privacy Policy is available online at www.eHarlequin.com or upon request from the Reader Service. From time to time we make our lists of customers available to reputable firms who may have a product or service of interest to you. If you would prefer we not share your name and address, please check here. ☐

HI07

Cut from the soap opera that made her a star, America's TV goddess Gloria Hart heads back to her childhood home to regroup. But when a car crash maroons her in small-town Mississippi, it's local housewife Jenny Miller to the rescue. Soon these two very different women, together with Gloria's sassy assistant, become fast friends, realizing that they bring out a certain secret something in each other that men find irresistible!

Look for

THE SECRET GODDESS CODE

by

PEGGY WEBB

Available November wherever you buy books.

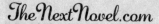
HN88146

HARLEQUIN®

INTRIGUE®

COMING NEXT MONTH

#1023 COLBY REBUILT by Debra Webb
Colby Agency
Shane Allen is a man unlike any Mary Jane Brooks has ever known. Maybe that's because he's a Colby man—and to save her life he'll have to become a human target!

#1024 THE MYSTERY MAN OF WHITEHORSE
by B.J. Daniels
Whitehorse, Montana
Laci Cavanaugh can't keep her eyes off new employer Bridger Duvall. Will they get the whole town talking about something besides weddings and murders?

#1025 CHRISTMAS COVER-UP by Cassie Miles
What's a sweet, talented woman like Rue Harris doing with tall, dark and gorgeous Cody Berringer? Give it some time and they'll discover their history started way before a Christmas murder—and miracle—brought them together.

#1026 THE CHRISTMAS CLUE by Delores Fossen
Five-Alarm Babies
Texas heiress Cass Harrison has a Christmas Eve rescue in mind. Can tough-as-nails FBI agent Matt Christiansen help her bring home an adorable baby girl to put under the tree?

#1027 MISTLETOE AND MURDER by Jenna Ryan
When a suspected murderer is paroled, ghosts from Christmas past haunt Romana Grey—and none so much as Detective Jacob Knight.

#1028 HONOR OF A HUNTER by Sylvie Kurtz
The Seekers
Everything Faith Byrne touches turns gold—except her love life. When a stalker goes to adjust that oversight, Noah Kingsley answers the call of duty to protect his first love and correct all of his past mistakes.

www.eHarlequin.com